BARCO

CW00544787

BARCODE

FIFTEEN STORIES BY **KRISZTINA TÓTH**

Translated from the Hungarian
by Peter Sherwood

JANTAR PUBLISHING

London 2023

First published in London, Great Britain, 2023 by
Jantar Publishing Ltd

Krisztina Tóth
Barcode

First published in Hungarian as *Vonalkód* by Magvető, Budapest, in 2006
English translation copyright © 2023 Peter Sherwood
Introduction copyright © 2023 Tímea Turi
Cover and book design © 2023 Davor Pukljak

A CIP catalogue record for this book is available from the British Library

ISBN: 978-1-914990-16-8

  Supported using public funding by
**ARTS COUNCIL
ENGLAND**

This book has been selected to receive financial assistance from English PEN's "PEN Translates"
programme, supported by Arts Council England. English PEN exists to promote literature and
our understanding of it, to uphold writers' freedoms around the world, to campaign against the
persecution and imprisonment of writers for stating their views, and to promote the friendly
co-operation of writers and the free exchange of ideas. www.englishpen.org

CONTENTS

CODED WRITING, PLAIN SPEAKING:
AN INTRODUCTION TO
KRISZTINA TÓTH'S *BARCODE*

R ARELY is the publication of a book in itself a literary event whose enthusiastic reception is subsequently confirmed by both readers and reviewers. In contemporary Hungarian literature Krisztina Tóth's collection of intriguingly linked short stories, *Barcode*, has proved to be such a volume: it has aged exceptionally well, even if ageing well happens to be one of the issues raised by the book, since for the characters in the stories the passage of time proves to be both a positive learning curve and a singularly destructive force.

CHRONOLOGY: THE BOOK

Krisztina Tóth was born in 1967 and the arc of her career as a poet – which is how she began – coincided with the end of the communist regime in Hungary: her first collection of poems was published in 1989 and her breakthrough came with *Porhó / Snowdust* in 2001. By the time her first book of short stories *Vonalkód / Barcode* appeared in 2006 she was already a celebrated poet. The evolution of her career, however, is another illustration of the familiar feminist charge that the literary emancipation of women is genre-dependent: that is, there are certain genres that are "more permissible" for women, poetry being one of them. While *Barcode* became a highly successful prose collection, it was precisely her outstanding achievements in poetry that hindered and yet simultaneously promoted the recognition of her work in prose, as is so often the case with women who write in multiple genres.

Its early reviewers invariably highlighted the similarities between *Barcode* and Krisztina Tóth's poetry, and while these certainly exist in terms of both language and vision, the prose of *Barcode* is incontrovertibly the real thing, its stories being powerfully condensed in form and having great dramatic force.

THE TIME AND THE SETTING OF THE STORIES

The experiences recounted in the fifteen stories of *Barcode* are contemporary with those of the author's life. Many are stories of childhood in the 1970s and 1980s, and the end of communism comes just as the characters are off to university.

The Pencil Case begins: "In my schooldays the colour both of our gowns and our copybooks was indigo", and indeed we are always given the time and place of each story from up close and in personal, deftly sympathetic detail. The background is provided by the consolidation of the Cold War, with "goulash communism" creating relative prosperity in Hungary, known as "the most cheerful barracks in the socialist camp." A growing child may be unaware of this and of how the soul is deformed by confrontation with the powers-that-be and by an atmosphere bereft of freedom, yet that does not mean they do not encounter these in their own particular way. The system reveals itself in the adults' frustrated words and deeds, as well as in the interactions between the children.

The Pencil Case may not be explicitly about scapegoating, but it does tell the story of how a little girl feels obliged to plead guilty when caught up in a conflict at school, even though she is innocent. And in *The Castle* the incomprehensible stories of the grown-ups overheard by the children provide the backdrop to a socialist summer camp of the period, where the irresponsible sticklers for order who are in their charge bully them for no good reason into keeping their rooms tidy in the Kafkaesque castle of the title. In another story, the eloquent and enigmatic *The Fence*, the father's deliberately repressed dramatic past, which certainly relates to the 1956 Revolution, continues to haunt a family's life for decades, "like a latent disease". There is probably no other book in Hungarian literature that writes so revealingly and so powerfully of social relations on a communist-era housing estate: see, for instance, *Black Snowman*, or *Insulated Floor*. The sensuous descriptions in *Barcode* – of the atmosphere specific to a school changing room, say, or a canteen, or a playground – are rooted in their familiarity to the reader, while they are at the same time reports from a world lost long ago.

The university student of *Outline Map* is on holiday with her boyfriend when the TV announces the passing away of János Kádár, the First Secretary of the Hungarian Socialist Workers' Party from the crushing of the Revolution in 1957 until his death in 1989, and a leading figure of the era that bears his name. In *Outline Map*, however, his death is treated on the same, matter-of-fact level as the application of suntan lotion:

> Actually, I felt rather sorry for him. Sorry that I would no longer be hearing his name in the news bulletins, sorry that the land of our childhood would soon disappear [...] I was angry at my parents, I was angry at my teachers, I was angry at the Skála Budapest department store, but for some reason I wasn't angry at János Kádár, as if he had nothing to do with

the uniform school pullovers we all had to wear, or with everything going on in this country.

János Kádár has died, just a little more on my shoulder, yes, there, on the side. That's always where you burn most easily.

In *Barcode* personal stories are more important than the stories of history, not least because history's stories are themselves ultimately the sum total of personal ones. The book is an account of coming to terms with personal losses, as time unrelentingly piles loss upon loss: the death of a friend, a disappointment in love, a miscarriage – but the loss may itself be the passing of time, the passing of one's childhood and youth.

SUBJECTIVE TIME

Furthermore, in these stories time does not flow at an even pace. It sometimes passes too slowly – especially in childhood – and sometimes too fast – particularly in adulthood; and sometimes it comes circling back, like fashions in, say, swimsuits. Indeed, the volume itself has a circular structure: it begins with a visit to a man on his deathbed and ends with a visit to another. The melancholy and bleak experience of bidding farewell, of having to let someone go, is a recurrent motif.

Yet the most characteristic property of time is that it may stand still, especially in a crisis: in several of these stories the narrator feels as if her life has taken on the quality of a film in which she is able to observe herself from the outside. The shocks may be major or relatively minor – misunderstandings, break-ups, betrayals – but each is always a profound crisis for the narrator. They seem to become alienated from themselves and it is in fact this sense of alienation that helps them to cope with the particular crisis. In *"The Witch Has Three, Three Kids Has She"* a woman suddenly confronting her cheating husband recalls:

> In fact, the camera that continued to roll in my head independently of my conscious mind even registered that the woman had varnished toenails. The whole thing was like some improbable film, in which we happened to be playing the main roles, but had suddenly forgotten our lines, so this take would end up on the cutting room floor. There will have to be another take; this one wouldn't do.

The story *I Love Dancing* is also a tale of a betrayal. "I was in a daze as I held the receiver. On the balcony opposite my brain mechanically registered a woman with a ponytail in a yellow bathrobe as she put her bedding out to air." Elsewhere: "Suddenly someone could be heard speaking from my throat, as if I were dubbing a character in a film." Or: "Perhaps I hadn't understood him right, perhaps this isn't even happening to me, perhaps this is a film" (both in *Outline Map*). And in the airport ordeal recounted in *Cold Floor*, a groundless accusation prompts the reflection: "My voice sounds to me as if it were coming from outside my body. I feel ashamed." In *Take Five*, set in Paris, a young woman receives a compliment from her long-unseen suitor: "'Merci bien,' an alien female voice replied."

Sometimes, however, it is just such alien and alienating moments that make it possible to experience the present. In *The Pencil Case* time first slows down when the little girl is unjustly accused of the theft, but later, in a similar situation, this slowing down happens of its own accord, as she names herself and comes to see herself as guilty of a crime she has not committed. The "I" is merely "the body belonging to the name": this, too, can make one vulnerable, while at the same time "the name belonging to one" can be something powerful.

Vulnerability is a recurrent theme in these short stories: children are at the mercy of adults, adults at the mercy of their emotions, and everyone is at the mercy of their bodies and of time, while vulnerability to time expresses itself through the body. This is a destructive force, yet it also implies a capacity to change. The story *What's This Mark Here?* spans long years, even decades, of a woman's life and is organised not linearly but by means of associations. When the woman, now a mother, shows a photo of herself as a child to her son, he responds: "'But Mum, that isn't you, that's a little girl.' Indeed: am I really me?"

"AM I REALLY ME?"

The book also keeps us in a constant state of uncertainty as to whether we are reading the stories of a single person at various times, or of several different women at roughly the same time. With the exception of one piece (*Take Five*) the stories are monologue-like, in the first person singular. Whenever the reading of the stories in a linear sequence suggests the possibility that there is a single narrator, we suddenly come across something that dissuades us from taking such a view. At the same time, there are stories that offer a more vivid, biographical reading (*The Fence* tells the same story about the 1956 Revolution that the author later expands on in a biographical note), while others distance us from such a reading quite radically (*Ant Map* is the most strikingly different world depicted.) However, it probably makes little difference whether we read the stories as being about one life or several, or how much or how little they resemble that of the author. Indeed, what the book suggests is that because the lives of humans are shot full of fractures – in the same way as the life line is broken on the palm of *Outline Map*'s protagonist – we are ourselves the possessors of several life stories unrelated to each other. And it is precisely the resulting fragments that bind us together, that highlight our similarities – and not just those of the sisterhood of women.

How do these fragmented experiences relate to each other? What do the parallels reveal? The work that has gone into the crafting of this book in order to raise such questions is perhaps its finest achievement. It should be noted that such bravura skills of editorial craftsmanship also characterise the author's later writing, such as the masterfully constructed *Pixel* (2011, English translation 2019).

PLAYING GAMES WITH BOUNDARIES

Barcode is a book about boundaries and therefore also about the crossing of boundaries.

The first element of the Hungarian word for "barcode" translates as "line", which is the book's main, heavy-load-bearing, leitmotif. It recurs in the subtitle of every one of the stories, though with a wide range of connotations. These "lines" are invariably linked to the particular story as a characteristic motif that helps to organise the fragmentary elements of its plot into a narrative. The structure of the book, too, seems to construct a visual game out of the parallelism of lines, just as a barcode consists of many short thin lines in parallel.

What kinds of boundaries are treated in the stories?

A boundary or border is not only something that separates countries (*The Castle, Cold Floor, Take Five*). Sometimes the boundary is between life and death (*Vacant People*). On occasion, a teacher crosses a professional boundary by spilling a schoolgirl's secret (*Tepid Milk*). But a boundary is also crossed when a dog takes on the fate of its owner, becoming as it were a surrogate victim (*The Fence*). At the same time, however, boundaries and lines not only restrict us but also provide us with security, as the endless rows of houses on an estate are paralleled by the lines in schoolchildren's copybooks (*Black Snowman*).

The second half of the compound, "code", offers just as important a linking motif: the stories seem to be driven by the desire that it is, perhaps, ultimately possible to decipher the world's hitherto mysterious interconnections. The opening lines of the final story, ("One way or another, even if it should come apart at the seams, the world is a web of sometimes opaque laws"), allude to the Hungarian poet Attila József's great poem *Consciousness* ("by and by, the weft of law is torn, unseaming"). While József's work embodies the experience of modernity's fragmentedness, Krisztina Tóth's characters here try to create a new order out of their fragmented stories. It is as if we were reading about the everyday, yet heroic, struggle to put things in some sort of order.

The title of the collection thus alludes not only to the everday sense of "barcode"– though in *Tepid Milk* it also does so explicitly: "The touchstone of things that came from the West was the barcode: those little black lines [...] that transformed objects into messengers from a world beyond our reach." And it is that story that is the key to the interpretation of the book's title. The high-school girl writes secret messages in the margins of her textbook in a script that only looks like the lines of a barcode but can be read as words when seen from the right angle: "to decipher it, you had to look at it from a different angle."

UNTRANSLATABLE PUNS

The language of *Barcode* is as dense as that of poetry. Even when it seems to be simple it is woven from a web of motifs that are carefully and delicately structured: it is a great virtue of the English translation that it appreciates and successfully re-creates this. Moreover, this dense prose is full of untranslatable puns. In the more fortunate instances the two languages are parallel, as in the ambiguity of the phrase "(to be) present" in *The Pencil Case*: the children mechanically respond with the word "Present" at morning assembly, while they are not "present" in their own lives. The title of *"The Witch Has Three, Three Kids Has She"*, a well-known Hungarian nursery rhyme (a literal translation would be "There's one witch") has been transposed to emphasise that she has three kids, since the mother in this story is raising her young son alone as she comes to terms with the loss of twins. Elsewhere, however, the English language serendipitously offers a connection not found in the original: *Outline Map* in Hungarian would translate more literally as "blind map".

SOUL AND FORM

Many of these stories could be told in a more serious register: the little girl in *Ant Map* is brought up by an irresponsible grandmother; the adolescent girl of *The Castle* has parents unfit for the task; the story of the miscarriage and break-up in *"The Witch Has Three, Three Kids Has She"* verges on the melodramatic. The stories are nonetheless neither overwhelming nor depressing: the careful attention to detail, the delicately etched scenes and relationships, make the narratives moving and memorable. The dramatic in these stories is frequently counterpointed by a detached and wickedly blasé sense of humour. Perhaps the most characteristic feature of *Barcode* is its unabashedly poetic tone, the way it maintains the tension between the narrators and their fate.

The most powerful metaphor for the style of the collection is nevertheless provided by the jewellery made out of the mysterious material found on the housing estate. The narrator of *Black Snowman* finds some "strange, curiously light, sponge-like stones gleaming with an oily sheen that reflected every colour of the rainbow", from which she makes jewellery and other beautiful, intricate objects that she showers on the residents of the estate. Only later does it transpire that this material is highly toxic waste, blast furnance slag. This is perhaps the most striking aspect of Krisztina Tóth's literary achievement: that whatever her raw material, she can fashion it into a thing of beauty, revealing the darkling, mysterious splendour of its radiance.

TÍMEA TURI

BARCODE

FIFTEEN STORIES BY KRISZTINA TÓTH

*This translation is dedicated to the memory of
my beloved mother, Rose Sherwood (1919–2009)*

VACANT PEOPLE

(BORDERLINE)

I was meant to be going down on the Thursday, but in the end I couldn't find the time. I didn't make it to Kecskemét until the Sunday and I was far too late to bid him farewell. There were four people surrounding the body when I arrived. Though it was a sweltering summer, they hadn't opened the windows, as if ashamed, even in each other's presence, of the sickly smell that was only intensified by the steamy warmth drifting in from the kitchen.

I looked at him in some confusion, reflecting on how the dead resembled one another, even at this stage, immediately after death, let alone later. Strangely enough, I can no longer recall the pain I felt, just as I can't remember the business that seemed urgent at the time and which made me arrive late. I remember only my unease as I shifted awkwardly from one foot to the other behind the distraught but taciturn relatives. I stood in the same posture, hands clasped in front of me and gaze vacant, as if some solemn speech were in progress, just as I had as a child when that dead, sallow-faced old lady was laid on the platform bench in the underground. That had been an old lady, this was an old man. Or rather, now, a non-entity, a vacant house, a hollow puppet, who had returned to the dwelling place of the soul.

There were sixty years between us. By the time I last saw him alive, three weeks before that late, and last, visit, he could barely speak. Curiously, in parallel with his long-drawn-out and then suddenly worsening condition, it seemed that the house and garden, too, began to show signs of falling apart. The lace tablecloths looked exactly the same, the door was propped open by the red kitchen stool just as before; yet something had nevertheless changed: the discreet choreography of arrivals and departures was different, the food tasted unfamiliar, dirt had lodged in the crevices of the handles of the knives and forks, and a strange smell pervaded the rooms. Especially his. He lay wrapped in a plaid blanket on an adjustable, metal-framed bed. I was surprised at how small his body was and how jagged and sharp its contours; by contrast, his speech was soft and crumbly, as if the words had lost their definition. He seemed to be communicating solely by his looks and especially his damp, glistening, blue eyes, now bulging out enormously.

"How long are you staying?"

I eventually understood what he was saying. I didn't want to lean any closer, as I found the smell of the medicaments and the talcum powder distressing, quite apart from the saliva that had gathered at the corner of his mouth. I had no wish for a close-up view of the skull faintly visible through his skin.

"I can't stay," I said, shaking my head.

He closed his eyes, as if reflecting on my reply. I didn't ever stay: I always came in the morning and took the evening train back, so I didn't really understand why he was asking. As if he didn't know I had to return.

Then, unexpectedly, he looked up and gestured to me to come closer. I rose from the chair and held an ear to his lips. What I heard was improbable in the extreme. At first I sensed only the rhythm of the sentence, something like "cover me up", but then as I glanced at his face and saw his look, I realised that he had indeed said what I heard.

"Give me a kiss."

I was caught in an uncomfortable position, above him and bent almost double, as he clutched my arm with one hand, longingly and with supernatural strength. I straightened up, removed his hand, and sat down again.

Without replying, as if I hadn't heard anything.

Sixty years between us; he could have been my grandfather. And in a sense that's what he was: I had listened to his stories, I had admired his pictures, I had sought his praise. And now here I was sitting beside him, horror-struck and ashamed, staring out of the window. For heaven's sake, what could he be wanting. I was 20 years old, an ignorant, know-it-all semi-adult. I didn't understand what he had in mind, whether it was a goodbye kiss, as if we were on a station platform with the train about to depart, or if it was not from me, a woman, that he wanted a kiss, but from someone in the land of the living that the one about to die wanted some parting gift, something wonderful but impossible – and that someone just happened to be me.

Meanwhile Aunt Edit had come in. She plumped up the pillow under his head, straightened the blanket, and asked if she shouldn't open the window. My little baby, she called the old man, something that even before I'd found weird and now seemed downright embarrassing, because if his wife was the mother of this sick and aged body, what did that make me? I was on edge, as if I'd been caught out doing something naughty. I knew little about living with someone and even less about being taken away from them, or at least too little to suspect that she wanted the same thing as her husband, that they had forever been one person in two bodies and it was just that one body would now remain lying there while the other went to the dining room to lay the table and serve the steaming hot soup.

We wielded our spoons in silence. As I looked into my bowl, I saw at once that something was not right. But I didn't dare say anything; it was simply out of the question. Beads of sweat formed on my brow and I felt increasingly nauseated as I tried to stir the soup in such a way that the tiny little insects floating in it ended up outside the spoon, but I couldn't do it, the odd one or two always remained and it would have been agonisingly awkward to pick them out with my fingers. Oh my God.

"Don't you like it, my dear?"

All I can remember, thinking back, is reaching for the toilet chain and noticing the yellowish tide-mark of the limescale in the bowl as I tried to vomit it all up: death, the smell of the herbs, the soup, everything, and, as I rested my brow against the wall, I shouted: no problem, I'm fine, it must have been the very early start and the journey down.

Now I'm standing in another bathroom, looking into a round mirror in a white frame which reveals my face, now 15 years older, as I gradually lower my towel. I am 35, I know something about birth, but still frighteningly little about death or, rather, that's how I feel, that's why I had to splash my face with cold water: to stop myself from bursting into tears.

A friend of mine has died.

It was a slow, difficult death, a gradual shrinking away, even as the child by my side continued to grow.

Best not mention the lower half of the body, so tiny and wrapped in a nappy.

Now he's lying over there in the room, his loved one by his side, or rather his loved ones, sitting there, holding his hands, smoothing his brow. I go back to the double bed; the girl on the left is crying. I sit down and look on, I say my goodbyes, though only to myself. The girl says to take his hand: it's already gone cold, but it's still warm under his armpits, that's where the spirit is still lurking, that's where its final refuge lies, from where it will leave for the very last time. That is its *home-pit*. And in fact I do put my hand there, gently, as if the three of us were just sitting around someone who was asleep, even though the sleeping body is vacant, the spirit having returned to its final refuge. There was no age difference between us, it could just as well have been me, yet I'm alive, alive. I have a son, I have a son, I have a son.

He's four. I squat down to hear what he's saying. For some reason he always calls the homeless 'vacant people'. Every morning in the Blaha Lujza underpass he sees the stinking bodies of the wretches snoring away on the cardboard boxes. I can see it pains him, that he doesn't think it's right, though this sight is part of his life, so much so that we generally stop and exchange a few words with Robi, who is often to be found in the mornings not far from our block, rifling through the giant wheelie bins.

"Why vacant?" I ask.

The underpass is busy, I'm crouched down by him, the crowd almost sweeps us away. He thinks for a moment.

"Because they haven't any locks," he replies.

I think I get it. I stand up and we go on. They have no doors, hence no locks on their non-doors, so they are vacant. I can't be sure that's what he means, but he will say no more, his lips are sealed. My little baby.

We come across Robi every day around eight, hard at work among the wheelie bins. Robi is in a wheelchair which he uses to roll right up to a container and when he is close enough, he swings forward to raise its lid and with his two muscular arms lifts himself out of the chair. For Robi has no legs. His shoulders are preternaturally broad: he grips the side of the container with one arm and with the other he starts rummaging about. If he finds anything, he throws it out, later using a stick to root about in the pile and see if there's anything that can be made use of. He would hang on like this for a minute or two, then flop back into his chair, exhausted, his arms trembling. When he lifts himself up, there's an occasional flash of his stumps. The back of his trousers is stained; obviously he can't always get out in time. One summer when the caretaker had washed out the containers and they were drying with their lids flung back, I was about to throw out some cat litter. The wheelchair was there but no sign of Robi. When I leaned into the container I suddenly recoiled from the damp, rank smell. Robi was standing inside the container, or rather, he would have been, if he'd had something to stand on. He was inside it, leafing through old copies of *Playboy*. I almost dumped the cat litter over his head. He gave me a fright. I asked him what he was doing there, to which he replied, cool as a cucumber, without even looking up, that he was reading.

"Can you get out?" I asked. He looked at me so scornfully that it made me blush, not least because, though he couldn't have guessed, what flashed through my mind was that I ought quickly to take a picture: *Legless man in a wheelie bin*. You could easily live in one of these, he added as he went back to his reading matter. I could imagine it: a wheelie bin with a lock.

That had all happened in the summer, but now it's autumn and quite cool, leaves litter the pavement. Looking at the wheels of the wheelchair, I notice something different since yesterday. Robi has threaded fluorescent green and pink shoelaces through its spokes, so these merge into a colourful strip as he bowls along. It must have been a very fiddly thing to do, but it was worth it. My son is ecstatic and waves to Robi for a long time. As I say goodbye I reflect on the colour of Robi's face: it reminds me so much of someone. Or rather of something. Yes: it's the old man's dead body, his yellow skull. Robi has a skull-like face. He won't be with us much longer, certainly not by winter.

On Friday I have to go down to Kecskemét. I haven't been there for many years, not once since the Old Man died. On the train, though, I still have the feeling that it's him that I am going to visit. The landscape is autumnal, crows circle around, a mist hovers above the bare fields. As I watch the various shades of brown and grey, and the thick smoke swirling up from somewhere, I wonder where the boundary is, that borderline between life and non-life, between life and death, whether there is some kind of definite borderland at all. I wonder about the living and the dead, about how over the years I have learnt nothing, I've merely grown older, and I wonder what has happened to my self-esteem and what has taken its place, and about all the things that have not, in fact, changed and would still make it impossible for me to kiss goodbye to someone who was about to depart.

I miss the afternoon train back and have several hours to wait for the next one. I take a stroll in the park by the station, then sit down on a bench in the playground. A – no doubt – Sunday father is shivering as he keeps a watchful eye on his track-suited little boy, who is intently piling gravel onto the slide. From time to time the father snaps tersely at him to stop it, but the boy, who must be about the same age as mine, pays no attention. The man turns away, lights up, and cups his raw hands around his cigarette. I'm cold.

The boy grows bored of the slide game, climbs into a tunnel of many colours intended for children smaller than he is, and spends some time inside it before coming out. From his hands there dangles a tampon that he takes over to his father. The man throws it away angrily, and they set off home.

I go into the waiting room, because it's getting dark and cold, and there's still a long wait for the train. I sit down on a bench: at least it's heated in here. I scan the adverts. A vagrant, leaning on a crutch, shuffles in, goes over to the white flip-top rubbish bin in the corner, and contemplates it at length.

On the side of the bin a freshly painted sign in blue proclaims: *This is Europe! Do not litter!* The vagrant undoes his fly and urinates into the bin; his aim is not entirely accurate. Hobbling over to a bench in the corner, he lies down, curls up, and falls asleep.

I'm still very cold, time drags by, I don't feel like reading; I'm tired. Slowly, I begin to envy the position the man's adopted. I stretch out on the bench and half drift off, head on my bag, arms crossed with my cold hands resting in my armpits, where it's warmest. After about ten minutes a railwayman comes in, plastic carrier-bag in hand. He looks round carefully, then switches off the fluorescent light.

Apparently, there's no one here.

THE PENCIL CASE

(GUIDELINES)

When I was at primary school the colour both of our gowns and of our copybooks was indigo. The vast building of the school was constantly steeped in the smell of the boiled vegetables percolating upwards from the kitchen, melding with the stale odour of children's bodies and gymshoe-rubber. Since despite its size the echoing, neon-lit, barn-like hall on the ground floor was not big enough to serve the needs of the hundreds of students, whenever several classes were timetabled for PE at the same time, one group was obliged to do the staircase run. We would have to race single-file up the right-hand side of the building to the second floor, then along the wide, apparently endless corridor that connected to the stairs at the back, and then down the stairs on the left-hand side. As we repeated the exercise six, seven, eight, nine times, until the double session of PE came to an end, the monotony of the grey steps of artificial stone blurred into a single, seemingly endless escalator and a curtain of stinging sweat descended over our eyes. Recurring patterns and worn treads marked each round, six, seven, eight, nine, I would see that gap for the sixth time, that step with the broken edge coming round for the seventh, the carved dog's head on the banisters the eighth time round, the cradle-shaped recess on the ninth. On the upper floor we could all take a few seconds' breather before tackling the back stairs, as by then even the best runners would be wheezing a little, but by the tenth time round no one could be bothered to stroke in passing the shiny, worn-down head of Sándor Nógrádi's bronze bust, so handily wedged in an upstairs alcove.

Afterwards we all lined up in the schoolyard: Class, atten-SHUN! Calves pinkish-white, cheeks almost the colour of mulberry, socks at half mast. The girls clutched their sides, the boys swore, Gulyás spat on the concrete. Line UP! The tips of the gymshoes lined up between the two big chestnut trees. Well done! As you were... class, dis-MISS!

The roots of the tree on the right, the one closer to the dining hall, had pushed up the concrete, and in the cracks there grew a few stalks of straggly grass, which I would poke the ants with during break. That was where Rudas had tripped last year. We were playing tig, running around the tree-trunk, which was a good three feet around, and I ran over to the far side, where above the high brick wall you could see the balconies of the block of flats next door. Roland Rudas suddenly popped out from behind the tree, a forest of children's hands reached out to touch his clothes and he suddenly swerved, obviously intending to change direction, but lost his balance and fell flat on his face. He stood up at once, looked around and seemed about to burst out laughing, but as he opened his mouth you could see from a long way off that his face was covered in blood. I watched, stunned, as he was surrounded by an ever-growing crowd proffering paper hankies, while he kept turning this way and that as he clutched his mouth. I watched the commotion as if it were some slowed-down silent film in which

I happened by chance to know all the actors. The tooth he had chipped later acquired a large, yellowish crown that didn't at all match his still-baby teeth. Once, when I ran into him as a grown-up, I scanned his face for the flaw I remembered, but the irregular, dull-looking tooth that was a feature of his smile after the accident was no longer there.

Who tripped up Rudas? asked the teacher, Miss Vera. We suddenly all fell silent, twenty frightened children all looking at each other wondering what would happen next. Rudas raised his head, his face a smear of blood and tears, and looked us up and down, paused for a moment, his glance bobbing to and fro the way a leather football might bounce between two stone walls facing each other. We stood in a circle as his glance continued to hover about uncertainly above our heads, before it settled on me. It really was like a still from a film: we stared at each other's faces through the empty ether, but I felt nothing, unless that there are stories and there is also fate, and a particular fate sometimes has no connection at all with the stories themselves, that fate has its own stories and its own time, and that this particular time had come to a standstill, with only my heart pounding very fast – no longer because I'd been running, but rather because of that something I've just called fate but which at the time I didn't call anything at all: it was more a sort of inkling, a feeling that refused to let me either lower my gaze or allow it to be caught during a moment that seemed to last for ever. Then the boy unexpectedly raised his hand in the air and pointed at me. I heard my name, at the sound of which all I normally had to do in class was stand up and say: Present. This, then, is the present, this improbably vast schoolyard, with its chestnut trees and the hand pointing at me through the ether, the name that would for ever and amen designate the person that had tripped up Roland Rudas, the person who remained stubbornly silent, and continued to stare at those ramifying tree roots, because she could never imagine that what they were told in biology was true, that beneath the surface of the ground a tree has roots as extensive as its crown. She could never imagine this mirror-image world, like the faces on playing cards, or how the gnarled labyrinth might reach down through the rich, subterranean loam, a netherworld of inverted foliage, teeming with insects and larvae. Later, too, the body belonging to the name continued to say nothing, responding with an obstinate silence and a blank, unflinching stare to the teacher's interrogation, and as for the name, she began to bear it as casually and forgetfully as her cardigan and the PE kit she invariably left behind somewhere or other. She became an actor in that weird film witnessed in the schoolyard, which the *I* had seen and in which *she* had been found guilty, and which from this day on I, the name, had constantly to bear through all the indigo days that followed.

In singing class I had to chant the name that belonged to me. I found it ridiculous and humiliating; I had no singing voice at all, but I sang it out when called upon to do so. And I was indeed called upon: my turn came after Szatmári's. Lying on top of each other on the bench were Kodály's *The Pentatonic Scale* and *333 Exercises in Reading Music*. There will be choir practice today, Mr Ossie said, all three classes will stay behind. We'll go down to the gym.

Everyone left their things upstairs and squeezed in among the vaulting horses and the rolled-up rubber mats. We made quite a racket as we waited; some people began to climb the wall bars, and even a medicine ball came trundling out from somewhere. We were having to prepare for the end-of-year concert: of all the schools in the district, ours had been accorded the honour of performing in the Red Star Cinema before the prizegiving. Class, atten-SHUN! Fall in! It's impossible to rehearse here, we'll go back upstairs after all and just bring in some chairs from the other classrooms.

We went back and I sat down at one of the desks at the back of the class. There were a lot of us and it took a good fifteen minutes for everyone to file in with their chairs and find themselves a space. Mr Ossie hung about in front of the open door, and the other teacher of singing, Miss Magdi, stood beside him, with Kinga Janák, from class C. For some reason they didn't come in. Everyone knew Kinga: her father was a well-known politician. He often came to our school to join the headmistress for wreath-layings, and Kinga had all kinds of stuff that very few in our class A had. A digital watch, scented erasers, copybook sleeves of coloured plastic: all things her daddy had brought her from abroad. And she owned a magnetic pencil case, something that in our class only Márta had. In fact, news of the magnetic pencil case reached us before the actual case itself, and for some reason I imagined that the way it worked was that you had to put the pencils in it with a magnet. But no: it was a plastic box with a lid that closed magnetically. Inside it was divided into compartments, separate ones for pens, pencils, and eraser. The shiny plastic lid had a picture on it, a yellow duck on Márta's, on Kinga's a Walt Disney Snow White, with the seven dwarfs. It was impossibly gorgeous, fabulously elegant. And the way she packed her things up at break! When we went into their class she would drop her pen in and click the lid down with the studied elegance of those women who slipped their sunglasses back into their little faux-leather cases. She also had a pink box for her paper hankies, and of course lip-balm, which she applied like lipstick during break, peering into her compact.

Why aren't they coming in? Mr Ossie popped his head round, his face looking very grim. Then in they came, Indian file, Kinga between the two teachers, bag in hand. They stopped at the front, surveyed the three classes, and after the atten-SHUN!, we had to remain standing.

Something extremely serious had happened, he said. Something of concern to us all, he was sorry to say. A sad and shocking event that we must now, all of us, deal with at once, since only the three Year 5 classes were here when we went down to the gym. Kinga Janák's pencil case has disappeared. It's been stolen.

Well, that put paid to the rehearsal. We sat in the classroom in total silence, and Mr Ossie walked up and down non-stop, talking all the while. The culprit is sitting here among us. If they admit what they have done, they can count on the others' understanding and forgiveness. We all have our moments of weakness, but with appropriate self-discipline, self-criticism and faith in the community, such temptations can be overcome. Because we are generally aware of how we ought to behave. What the guidelines are. But on occasion even the most disciplined of students can stray. We all make mistakes, weakness as such is not unforgivable, but if we heap further lies upon the foul deed, we may forever forfeit the trust of our fellows and our teachers. Though he could have gone easy on the culprit by offering them a chance to put the pencil case on the teacher's desk after class, he would rather give the thief the opportunity to ask for the forgiveness of the community as a whole. To exercise self-criticism in front of all of us. We are none of us leaving here, said Mr Ossie, until the pencil case turns up.

The singing rehearsal was cancelled; we sat behind the firmly closed windows. I don't want to hear a pin drop! So who was it? I have plenty of time, I've had my lunch. An hour passed and in the dining hall the plastic jugs continued to stand, the soup continued to get cold, as we sat with hands behind our backs and the bell went not just once but twice. Very well, said Mr Ossie, if that's the way you want it, so be it. If anyone knows who the culprit is and is covering up for them, they too are guilty of a crime and deserving of the community's contempt.

I have plenty of time. By the way, lunch today was poppy-seed pasta, I'm sure none of you like that anyway. Year 6 is out in the yard, you too could all be out there playing football, if you came to your senses. Stop that scribbling or I'll break your arm. A propelling pencil? I'll take that, thank you very much, you can have it back at the end of term.

Well? Any ideas?

Kinga Janák was sitting at the back, looking as apprehensive as the rest of us, and you could see that she was now regretting the whole pencil case business. The air in the hall was oppressive, we were all sweating, and more and more people were asking to be excused. Mr Ossie timed every trip, to ensure people returned from the toilet within the allotted two minutes. Motes of dust glinted as they danced in the air. I examined carefully the back of my hand, then the notches carved in the bench, the cross-stitching of the curtains, the spiderwort, pale and largely bereft of leaves as it sat in its blotchy pot. The heavy heat of May flooded in through the windows, the hubbub from the far side of the yard and the noises of the street merged with the protracted, headache-inducing silence indoors; the wrought iron pot holder, the record player stand, the blackboard were all unbearable, as unbearable as the amorphous green pattern that repeated at eighteen-inch intervals on the lino, as unbearable as the present, the future, the past, my chanted name on the copybook labels, as unbearable as the nauseating airless press, as our elevenses stuffed in their plastic bags, as the smell of nylon schoolgowns drenched in sweat, and the hot, chalkdust-filled air, heavy with the breath of eighty schoolchildren.

For the last time of asking, said Mr Ossie, glancing at his watch.

I had no idea what the time might have been, but I did somehow sense that time had come to a standstill, that the clock could never be turned back, that some mysterious force had buried us in the grip of an eternal present, and even if at that point none of this was articulated at all clearly in my head as it got steadily heavier, I did at least have the suspicion that the name that belonged to me had the power to bring to an end this moment frozen in time, that in the grand scheme of things the significance of the individual disappears, that whoever is guilty was born with that guilt, so that as far as their actions are concerned they are free because, do what they will, on the map of stories, they are bound always to follow the same path. That, who knows, it may well have been me. That perhaps at some point, in some other story, I did in fact do it. It seemed that an eternity passed before the alien body that belonged to me stood up, waited for every eye to be fixed on it, and said in my alien voice, so that the airless press of the present might at last come to an end and we might all go home:

It was me.

OUTLINE
MAP

(LIFE LINE)

"Which palm should I be looking at?" I asked, putting them side by side.

"How should I know," she replied. "Wherever it's longer."

She finished washing up, wrung out the sponge firmly, wiped her hands on the dishcloth, and left. I went over to the sink, intending to take a glass, but the dishes were drying at the end opposite to where I usually stacked them. I found everything about this kitchen annoying, everything was the wrong way round. The entire flat was aggressively dominated by my mother's left-handedness. The matches were on the left-hand side of the fireplace, the sponge was to the left of the sink, even the dishcloths were on the left, where she had indeed just hung up the wet one when she finished.

I'm quite certain not to live very long. The life line on my left palm is broken halfway along, and although it does continue lower down, almost as far as my wrist, not with the best will in the world could you say that it was unbroken: according to my girlfriend the gap was like a coma lasting several years, a kind of bracket, after which life carries on as before. There was no break in the one on my right palm, but the straight line was much shorter and branched off oddly at the end, like the split ends of a hair. I pondered what the branching off might mean: so, was it a coma or a gap, and when exactly? But not even my mother could say which palm was to be believed.

On her own left palm, too, there was a place where the line was broken and resembled mine.

I went back to my room, to return to the Age of Rome. I'd broken the back of the essay. The heat was oppressive. I sat on the floor, surrounded by piles of clothes and empty Coke bottles, trying to see if I could create some order among the papers using my toes, seeing if I could use them to turn the pages. I couldn't, got cramp in my foot, and had to get up and stamp my feet to get rid of it. This was my last exam, all that stood in the way of summer.

"Please don't cry, for heaven's sake, there really is no point."

I didn't know the teacher taking the oral. I no longer went to class very much in any case, as the subject didn't interest me. I was in love, and bored by the dates and the outline maps you had to fill with place names. I roamed the corridors of the university like an outsider, constantly losing my way and missing appointments, and I couldn't understand the point of it all, why you had to know where the medieval notarial places were, or where the Reformation texts were printed. I was terrified that one day they'd discover that I was here by some mistake. *I'm sorry*, they'd say, *but there's been a dreadful misunderstanding*. Let's learn Finnish, my girlfriend said one autumn morning, and we sat in on a man yelling in a six-fingered shaman's glove. Let's learn Hebrew, said my girlfriend one winter morning. Yes, let's! And for three weeks we really did. Then, one morning in spring she greeted me in the cafeteria with the words: I've found a rather good make of Polish foundation. Non-greasy? I asked, stirring my coffee, though in the past I'd in fact found Polish cosmetics to be rather good. In the end we didn't take Polish either, everything stayed the same, only my days would begin later and later, and by the end I was skipping morning classes entirely.

But now I really had to put in those bloody towns on the map. I stared at the lines drawn in Indian ink; one might have been a river, as it split into two at the bottom of the sheet. Slowly, almost against my will, my tears began to flow, coursing their way down my cheeks and landing on the sheet of paper, forming round little magnifying-glass lenses; beneath one there wound a thicker line, a river, or border, or whatever. I tried to wipe it off with a paper hankie, but that just made the splodge bigger.

I stared out of the window, past his head. Through the nylon curtains you could see the cars as they inched their way past.

He was a thin man, in his thirties, with a rather prominent nose. He looked rather miserable, with his long, tobacco-stained fingers and padded jacket. How shitty it must be, I thought, to have to sit here with me in this heat. I'm the last one, the very last; everyone else left for their holidays long ago. His mouth moves, the cars inch their way along. I simply switched off the sound, leaving just the frame of the window to watch, and as I slowly turned away, the side of his face and one ear still hung into the frame. He managed to stay cordial and calm, treating me as a problem to be solved, a test of his patience, a sulphurous punishment of God's that he had to accept in all humility and without questioning the will of fate.

"Don't cry, please don't."

Suddenly the sound came on.

"Why won't you say anything?"

I stared at him as if I were surprised to find myself sitting somewhere like this, amidst this varnished furniture, on this faux-leather chair, then suddenly someone could be heard speaking from my throat, as if I were dubbing a character in a film. It piped up and said:

"I don't want any of this."

Out in the corridor I could sense he was nearby, waiting for me. I loved him so much that I could feel his presence anywhere, I simply knew he must be there. I checked myself and turned round. He looked me in the eye.

"It's cool. No problem. You'll do a re-take in September."

I ate the sandwich he'd brought; wrapped in the plastic bag since the morning, it tasted a bit like the elevenses we used to take on our class trips. He had cut the hot bits out of the green peppers.

"Tastes good."

We sat on the bench in the corridor, like people waiting for a train. He too seemed exhausted.

I told my mother I postponed the exam, and that we were going away. I'll do a re-take in September.

"You know best," she said.

All my life there were three sentences that I most often heard her say: *you know best, I've nothing more to say,* and *pull yourself together*.

You know best would generally be followed by a *but*, though she was capable of giving that *you know best* a vast range of threatening and blackmailing overtones that my ears, having been brought up on them, were immediately able to interpret, distinguishing between simple dislike and express disapproval. If there was a serious problem, this was conveyed with somewhat greater explicitness; I mean, if she had to put down for a moment whatever object she happened to have in her left hand, be that scissors, wooden spoon, perhaps the telephone receiver, then this would generally be followed by *I've nothing more to say.*

Like in a sports quiz on TV: "So now for your questions on sports. Tell me, madam, do you watch the sports broadcasts? Perhaps together with your good husband? I've nothing more to say. Think carefully, madam, if you haven't, that's fine, we'll just go on to the lucky dip."

The third sentence was *pull yourself together*. As if talking to a child who has yet again thrown their Lego all over the place: go and pick them all up. There was something defensive about this (it's not my Lego, you're the one who was playing with it) and also something threatening (I'm going to throw every piece of your Lego out in a minute!); but there was also an element of reproach (you know, I never had any Lego when I was your age). Pull yourself together, take the rubbish out: the tone was just the same, as if she were saying: stop picking your nose.

"We're going down to Lake Balaton," I said to my mother and didn't wait for her reaction.

"We're going down to Lake Balaton," he said to his mother. We happened to be face to face with her buttocks, somehow addressing her rear end, because she was standing on top of the toilet seat, with a roll of woodgrain-pattern self-adhesive wallpaper in her hands.

"By all means, my dears. We're all dying of heat here anyway." And she went on covering the cistern with the wallpaper, as that didn't fit in overall. Everything in the flat was brown and white, as was the fashion at the time: the three piece suite had a brown-and-white striped cover, the cushions in the dining room were brown-and-beige, in the bathroom the rim of the beige bath was lined with brown bottles and boxes of shampoo and bath salts. But somehow the toilet cistern didn't match. Now that she'd been left alone in the flat (her husband, that is to say, my beloved's father, having announced a few days earlier that he was going off on his own – *you know best*, she'd responded without turning round and continued attending to the flowers on the balcony), so, now that she was alone in the empty flat, she'd repainted the flower pot holders and bought a roll of self-adhesive wallpaper.

She clambered down and surveyed her handiwork from out in the hallway. It looked quite dreadful, with the wallpaper all crinkled at the corners. She'd added a patch but it failed to match the pattern of the woodgrain.

"It's spot on," said my beloved, and I felt a pang of envy at the family, the two of them, mother and son, as they eyed the cistern, your father won't notice a thing, 'course he will, it looks so much better, from a distance you really can't tell it's crinkled.

"Off you go, my dears. Just take care!"

We lay in the musty darkness of the summer cottage watching TV. There were pieces of woven fabric all around the bed; on the table a black Korond vase and an ashtray with a condom wrapper in it.

It was 32 degrees; we slathered each other in suntan lotion as we watched the TV. The General Secretary of the Hungarian Socialist Workers' Party János Kádár has died. Actually, I felt rather sorry for him. Sorry that I would no longer be hearing his name in the news bulletins, sorry that the landscape of our childhood would soon disappear, that the crêperie shack on Kálvin Square had been demolished and that entire blocks of houses were disappearing, that the streets twisted and turned in odd directions, that in the sequence of events some kind of curious, unbridgeable gap was being created. The first time we met we were still able to sit in the crêperie shack on Kálvin Square, but it was demolished soon after. Gaps suddenly appeared in its bare but homely walls, and through the gaps a brighter but unknown and frightening world was revealed, one which we couldn't imagine ever having access to. I was angry at my parents, I was angry at my teachers, I was angry at the Skála Budapest department store, but somehow I wasn't angry at János Kádár, as if he had nothing to do with the uniform pullovers we all had to wear, or with everything going on in this country.

János Kádár has died, just a little more on my shoulder, yes, there, on the side. That's always where you burn most easily.

I remember another year, some time later, sitting with another man, in the same way, in some resort, another man that I loved but who no longer loved me, and behind whose head the turned-down TV showed the bridge at Mostar in flames. The picture of the head of state was on the screen for a long, long time, there were moles on both sides of his face, the kind wolfhounds have, even ours.

The day after János Kádár died my beloved said: let's go out for dinner. He wanted to discuss something. What he meant was that he had something to tell me.

As I dried my hair in the bathroom, I watched the image in the round mirror and switched off the sound. The tip of the orange-coloured dryer went around my head like the prowling fox in a puppet show. *"Clippity-cloppety, yum-yum, here is the feast and then yum-yum, he swallowed the lot. Tell me a story, Uncle Remus!"*

"You ready to go?"

We sat in the restaurant; he was behaving somewhat oddly, perhaps a touch too politely. Then he relaxed, and even smiled now and then. At the table next to us sat three lads, swearing away non-stop. It was quite a feat, replacing every other word in every sentence with fuck, *fuck knows what the fuck that fuck wanted.* As we listened to them we burst out laughing, they're *fuckraking*, we said, we liked that, laughed about it for a while, then he gave an unexpected frown and laid down his fork.

"Listen."

I was listening.

"This whole thing. I can't take it any more."

Mechanically I continued to push the crêpe around the plate with the back of my fork, drawing lines in the melting chocolate sauce. Rivulets began to flow, winding their way along the white plate, *what IS this, what IS this.*

"Oh, please don't cry," he said awkwardly. I sat on the lid of the toilet and sobbed as I leant against his stomach. I don't remember how we got home, only the sudden realisation, still in the restaurant, that perhaps I hadn't understood him right, perhaps this isn't even happening to me, perhaps this is a film with the waiter going to and fro and there are people just sitting all around us.

I was still leaning my head against his stomach as he rhythmically, awkwardly stroked my hair. I suddenly lifted my face and turned away, and there it was, Veronika's scarf, above it across the chest an improbable logo: "Swimming across Lake Balaton".

"Why didn't you tell me before?"

"Because of the exams."

"And why now? Why the fuck did you have to bring me down here? Why didn't you come with her? Why? Why? Why? *Why?*"

I've nothing more to say. He looked away, up into the air, out of the toilet window, as intently as if he could discern something in the foliage of the cypresses out there in the dark.

I clutched my stomach as I sat on the toilet, as if I had stomach ache, while he stood above me, and then after a while he said: *I'm sorry.* (I'm sorry, but I'll just have to take this Lego away. It was only given to you on loan.)

For a long time the sound cut out, the rocking motion lasted a little longer, as if I were being shaken in a comfy cooking pot lined with cotton-wool, up and down, up and down, like the time in my childhood when we collected ladybirds in little glass jars, *ladybird, ladybird, fly away home, your house is on fire, your children are gone,* what's that strange smell.

"Why won't you say anything? Did you hear what I said?"

I did. I didn't reply. I looked past the doctor's head, out of the window, surely this will soon all be over. Two weeks of improbable dreams, I hover silently above sounds and conversations, swathes of linen, the ladybirds shaken up and down inside the glass jar, I'm a river, I've become a river, there's no sea for me to make for.

"How are you feeling?"

I say nothing, I'm not feeling at all, I just stare. A pause, a dull, soundless band an inch or so above one wrist. Got it: so it's the left one, after all.

In our family, everyone – apart from me – is left-handed.

My mother is sitting by my bed. She tries to take my hand, the one nearest to her. The right one is anyway bandaged up, with the drip in it.

Pull yourself together.

I stare at the creases on the blanket, a great, big white outline map, you have to fill in the towns on them, but where, where on earth, can they be.

And anyway, what is this country?

THE FENCE

(BLOOD LINE)

I scrambled downstairs in my pyjamas. My parents were already up. The scene was weird and scary at the same time. We stood blinking under the garage's striplight, staring at its head. Because that was all you could see, the head that it had forced through the cat-flap while chasing the cat. And though it had managed to push the flap in, when it tried to pull its head out, it had got hopelessly stuck: neither in nor out. The fur around its ears was covered in blood. My mother grabbed hold of the dog and started pushing it from behind. No luck. Then she tried to coax it to pull its ears back and squeeze through, but the angle was impossible. All the squealing had by now woken up the neighbours, who were out on the upstairs balconies with their lights turned on.

"Hey, mind the garage door! Leave it the fuck alone! Just cut it off!"

"You mean cut its head off?" My father, incredulous, turned in the direction of the voice. The neighbour was shivering in his dressing gown and just wanted the noise to stop. My mother burst into tears and kept kicking and pushing the door and then, for some reason, wrapped a blanket round the dog, thinking it might be cold.

"You think she might be thirsty?" she asked.

My father was beside himself at the dog: "Fucking stupid bitch!" In the end, the next-door neighbour, a joiner by day, rustled up a chainsaw, and they set to work. My mother held the tightly wrapped body from behind, while I squatted down next to it in the doorway. I tried to calm the creature, but there was no point: by then she was past hearing anything, whimpering away with her eyes rolled far back in her head, her drool flowing down onto the concrete. The sun was up by the time we finished.

"I'm going to murder that fucking cat," my father commented on the night's events as he put the chainsaw back by the boiler.

Still, in the morning that fucking cat turned up at the usual time for its raw liver, the only thing it had deigned to eat for some time now. It surveyed disdainfully the debris of the night's mayhem – the blanket and what remained of the garage door, by the wall – then padded over to my mother's feet to await the clink of its dish on the floor.

The dog, on the other hand, wouldn't eat. For two whole days it refused to come out from under the table and wouldn't let itself be touched. It trembled all the time, its nose was dry, and its eyes had an oily glow. Only its empty plastic bowl indicated that it was, nonetheless, prepared to drink some water. This was when, in my mother's opinion, the dig stopped growing – "from the shock", she claimed. Though to be honest, I had my suspicions about the dog even before this happened. A German Shepherd from prize-winning parents, fifth of the litter – but no proof of pedigree.

When we first brought her home, this whelp of prize-winning parents pissed all over my coat, only to spend the next two months rapidly and seriously getting stronger and growing – though, it should be said, only lengthwise. Its legs failed to get any longer and the dog as a whole began to resemble a dachshund, one that had been whimsically crowned with the head of a German Shepherd; its velvety antenna-ears were entirely out of proportion to the breed. The drunks hanging around the off-licence next door soon grew fond of the pup behind the railings with its high-pitched squeal, and kept shouting: "Shut the fuck up, bat-ears!"

By the age of one, it was as tall as it would ever get: mid-calf height. Its ancestry – since the owner of its parents with their distinguished blood line never again made an appearance at the market – remained shrouded in mystery: dachshunds, German Shepherds, retrievers, and fox-terriers chased after one another endlessly awhirl on this genetically obscure terrain.

The dog was forever hanging around my father, getting under his feet when he came rolling up with the wobbly wheelbarrow from the back garden, or burning piles of leaf mould. Even though she was afraid of the smoke and kept shaking her head and snorting and spluttering, there she would be again the next time he made the trip, sniffing around my father's rubber boots. In high summer they would relax side by side, but the dog was on the alert even when it was napping, and if it heard some suspicious noise would run grunting and wheezing over to the gate and then, alarm over, return to hunker down in the shadow of her master's belly.

My father had an enormous belly, criss-crossed by deep scars the colour of mother-of-pearl that were only partially covered by the blond hairs across his stomach and chest. One of the scars, the main trail, wound its way as far as his collarbone. It was traversed by three crossroads, one at the chest, another just above his navel, and a third lower down. On his back, too, there were two craters, sewn up with enormous stitches. My father had been covered with these mysterious trails since before I was born; they led deep inside him, into that dark and silent forest of which he never spoke. For our part, we never asked where these trails came from and where they led and simply acknowledged their existence: the story of the accident. How often had we heard the story of the car skidding on the icy road, spinning round and crashing into another as it spilled out all its passengers.

He had told this story any number of times, always with the same tried and tested turns of phrase, whenever anyone asked about those horrific scars – and people very often did. He'd played water polo in his younger days and even though in the showers he would try to grab a towel and cover up the scars, his teammates always ribbed him mercilessly: "Not the Grim Reaper after you, was it?" He would laugh along with them and say: "Yeah, it was, but he couldn't swim fast enough!" And he would have to tell the story of that icy road again, for the hundredth time.

In fact, these days only his broad shoulders would remind anyone of his water polo playing days, his belly having rounded out and expanded exponentially. For my father loved his food, guzzling down – indiscriminately and to excess – everything put in front of him, as if trying to make up for all the times he'd been left hungry as a child. In this respect he was very much like the dog, which also made sure that the chunks of meat it was fed disappeared in a flash, without even bothering to chew them, and if you tried to slow things down by serving up the food a little at a time, its pointed nose would sniff out and hoover up the surrounding terrain in seconds.

In the past it had managed to wolf down burst balloons, chunks of tennis balls, plastic watchstraps, even carrier bags. As the bags proved impossible to evacuate in the normal way, the vet had to scrape them out of the creature's blocked intestines after it had been retching for days on end.

No wonder she watched my father with great empathy, head cocked to one side, as he demolished his third helping of cabbage and pig knuckle, sweating profusely in the summer heat, and bent over the terrace handrail. "I'll be fine," he said, more to the dog than to my mother, as they both awaited developments. Then he somehow managed to drag himself indoors to lie down, but failed to surface even once the midday heat had passed. Or even by evening. On the contrary, he became increasingly shivery, had to wrap himself in several blankets, and kept moaning pitifully. My mother continued to change the icepacks as she reeled off, at great length and with much sighing, all the things my father ought not to have eaten to avoid the consequences that, as he could surely see, had now befallen him, and might indeed have befallen him much earlier, after the rabbit, the stuffed cabbage and the cheap booze that had been served up at Dezső's. All the while she kept bringing him bowls of water with increasing frequency, because by midnight the icepacks were melting in a matter of minutes. In the middle of the night he suddenly sat bolt upright, stopped moaning, and declared he wanted to make his will, at which point my mother decided to call for an ambulance.

The gall-bladder operation went without a hitch. My father felt better; we just had to wait for the results of the scan. They found shadows on his liver which had to be checked out. They might be cysts; we'd soon know for sure. A week later the doctor called my mother in. He asked her about that car crash long ago: what exactly had happened? It would be helpful if she could dig out the paperwork because the adhesions suggested that further intervention might be needed. My mother was alarmed by the word 'intervention', her nerves being further put on edge by the grim-faced doctor who looked her in the eye all the time, as if trying to catch her out. The shadows on the liver, the doctor remarked on his way out, appeared to be pieces of shrapnel, at which my mother stared at him blankly, either because she couldn't place the word 'shrapnel' out of context, or because she'd just realised she hadn't handed over the brown envelope she'd been clutching and outside, in the corridor, she no longer dared to. So, it would be good to get hold of the discharge note issued after the accident, because in my father's stomach they'd found some growths which were – and here he had looked at my mother again – distinctly odd and which we might be clearer about if we knew more about the circumstances.

He left the room, but my mother stayed sitting there for a while and only later went back into the ward.

"Dr Gyarmathy," my father managed to murmur, "but he may no longer be alive."

But Dr Gyarmathy was very much alive and greeted my mother wearing a white shirt and jacket. He was well into his nineties, but ramrod straight. Only later, after half an hour's conversation, did he start to play the role of the senile old man with memory loss – to my mother's mind, none too convincingly.

He hadn't been easy to find. He had retired to an out-of-the-way village, far from the border, and it had taken two weeks to track him down. Heaven knows how my mother managed to persuade him to meet up with her. Perhaps he did after all want to see what had happened to that loose end he had failed to tie up, the life that in the 1956 Revolution he had, in his utter desperation, unwittingly turned upside down.

"I can't remember," he said. "I'm really sorry, my good lady, but I just can't remember." Yet he remembered all too clearly: for years it had dominated his dreams, and whenever he heard steps on the pavement outside at night, or felt a shudder on a night call, he would think: That's it, the story continues, because he knew that stories never end, they only break off and lie low, like latent diseases, and then resurface and continue to spread, resulting in stabs of pain elsewhere, only for that pain to be passed down from generation to generation. And although he might sometimes be able to put a name to the disease and treat the resurgent pain, he didn't know what to do about those stories that circulated endlessly, as in the case of this woman: what on earth could he do for her? About the fragments of shrapnel lodged in the man's liver, about the decades of silence, the trauma that lingered on, ingrained?

There'd been fourteen of them, nine adults and five children. My father was thirteen at the time, the other kids a year or two older. But this was not obvious, because despite his size he was the most capable of them all, the one who'd always had to look after his six younger siblings, and gradually he grew to fill these shoes. He didn't stand out from the big lads, perhaps they didn't even realise he was younger. He joined the others because he'd heard that the West was the Promised Land. The borders were open, you could just leave. Throughout the chaotic days of the Revolution the family had stayed with relatives in a village near the border. At least there you were sure to get food even when the cities were running short. His mother, my grandma, didn't understand what was going on. Even before, she'd known precious little about politics: she simply brought one child after another into the world, and all the chaos and rowing in the family was driving her out of her mind. She did nothing but cook noodles in a big pot, and yell at the kids.

My father had had enough of looking after his brothers and sisters, enough of the noodles, of the rags they all went around in. He decided to escape with the others and set off for the border.

The group woke the local doctor at daybreak. They were village folk, a noisy lot, and rattled the windows. They said they'd been woken up around two in the morning by the sound of gunfire, but none of them dared go outside. They waited indoors in silence, whispering, guessing, praying, and then, in the grey light of dawn, the men got dressed and decided to take to the fields after all. Fourteen people lay on the ground, all young folk from nearby. None of them was breathing any longer, but there was a trail of blood across the frozen ground suggesting that one had tried to set off, perhaps for home, across the fields. They were shrouded in a pall of silence. Some lay face down, others on their backs, their clothes covered in the hoarfrost of the early dawn. There were no tears or wailing from the men or, oddly enough, even from the few women who dared venture out after them. They spoke in short, quiet sentences. The truck came and they piled on the dead. And when all the bodies were on the truck, you could see that one of the bodies stirred.

It was my father.

The men banged on the doctor's window: Do something! The very old man who'd stood facing my mother today was then a young doctor at the beginning of his career. He looked out: what on earth could they be wanting at this hour?

A wave of anger and despair swept over the men and seemed to be channelled towards the doctor, as if it was all his fault: "that rabble", they kept saying, and shot him such murderous glances that he almost began to fear the men in heavy boots pushing and shoving around him. It was the Russians, they shouted, they've closed the border.

My father still had a pulse. They carried him over to the summer kitchen; blood was oozing from his mouth and trailing along the stone flags at the entrance and into the inner courtyard. Lights went on in the nearby cottages, but the group ignored them and awaited developments in silence in front of the summer kitchen. The doctor called out to one of the men and together they carried the body into the house. "They've got to op'rate," one of the women reported back.

The operation was carried out on the dining room table. My father had been struck by four bullets: two had passed straight through him, the other two had lodged in his body. It was these that had to be located in the dim light of dawn, under a copper lamp. The doctor was short of instruments and short of time; they'd come almost too late as it was. By the time they finished it was nine o'clock. Dr Gyarmathy came out into the yard and appeared to be taken aback, as if he'd only just realised that there were people sitting and waiting by the wall.

"Go home, all of you. Go," he said, and wanted to add, as he usually did, that everything would be fine, but he didn't believe that himself.

"Shouldn't we tell his mother?" asked one of the women, but the doctor just shooed her away and ushered them all out of his yard.

After the operation my father ran a temperature; the doctor said it was a miracle he didn't die of sepsis. They took him over to Dr Gyarmathy's sisters, where he lay – as a 'relative' – for three weeks, during which his mother thought he'd fled to Budapest and was ready to *wring his sorry neck the minute he showed his face*.

Now, in his tenth decade, Dr Gyarmathy had no recollection of the forms he'd filled out afterwards. Even the name meant nothing to him: there must be some mistake, he kept assuring my mother as he showed her out, it was all so long ago. He'd help if he could, he really would. Then, as he opened the gate, he suddenly shot my mother another look and said: "I'm sorry. I'm frightened." Then he shut the gate.

So the papers about the car accident never turned up, but provided he followed a strict regimen a further operation could – for the moment, they said – be avoided. My father pottered about at home, forbidden to do any heavy lifting, but as the weeks turned into months he found doing nothing harder and harder to bear. He sat in front of the television all day long, watching the borders being reinforced. Hour after hour they showed footage of fanatical, stone-throwing foreigners storming the border fence. He nodded in approval: *A good thing, that fence. It'll protect us. Whoever came up with that had the right idea.* He was especially impressed by the razor wire. He decided to have his own fence repaired to protect his property. Not just because the dog was constantly barking and harassing passers-by – with my mother in constant dread that they'd give it rat poison to silence it – but also because of the litter left by the yobs hanging around the off-licence, the empty bottles and food wrappers they threw into our garden. He was fired up by the thought that at last he'd get everything sorted out properly. And anyway, he would add, no reason everyone should see into our backyard, it's not a cinema. What he had in mind was a high fence, solid stone, with six-inch nails on top.

My mother was against the idea: why did the house have to be turned into a fortress. But my father was adamant. He was so excited by the planning and the preparations that he more or less forgot about his illness and his medications. He felt invigorated, a young man again.

They totted up the figures: the fence cost a fortune. More than my father was expecting and more than he could afford. But he dug his heels in. That was the fence he wanted, and that was that. None of anyone else's business.

He talked things over with the workmen: they strode about purposefully, taking measurements, and he never brought up the cost again, as if it didn't matter.

Just make sure it's good and strong, he would keep saying, which really infuriated my mother: why did a fence have to be so damn strong, who'd be coming here with a tank, she'd say, but my father said nothing and stuck to his guns. He waved my mother away: really not someting she should stick her oar into.

When the stonemasons came, he opened up both wings of the wire-mesh gate to let them in. There were four of them, on a small truck, with a cement mixer and shovels and sacks. My father did think it odd that the dog didn't bark at them, but he put it to the back of his mind. He helped carry the tools and hump the smaller sacks, as if he'd deliberately forgotten about everything he was not supposed to do. He told the men to mind the grass and do their mixing only at the back, coming the longer way round with the wheelbarrow, and showed them where to ditch the dirty water. "And if it rains the tools could be put in here," he said, opening the green garage door, which had streaks of blood on the ground in front of it. The dog lay inside.

"And what's this?" asked one of the men.

My father stared numbly.

"It's done for," he said quietly, as if trying to explain to himself what he was seeing, totally at a loss, as if unwilling to check whether the body was still warm, as if unwilling to take it somewhere quickly, to do something, anything, as if he'd never seen it before, as if it weren't even his – ours –, as if he hadn't that very morning stroked that now completely lifeless little body.

"It's done for," he repeated, as if passing sentence over it, then rubbed his face vigorously and went off to tell the men what to do next. On his way he stepped into the trail of blood.

"We had one, too," one of them offered. "Kept dashing off, till it got run over by a car."

My father looked him up and down but said nothing. He turned away and hurried off to show them where they could dump the sand.

ANT MAP

(LINE OF PASSAGE)

Grandma always knew what the weather was going to be. Sometimes she didn't even leave her little house and just patted her midriff as she lay on the motley coloured cushions scavenged from the nearby rubbish dumps, and groaned: *Cold's a-comin'*. That little house of hers was packed to the rafters with all kinds of stuff. On the high bed covered with an orange faux-fur blanket sat rows of shabby teddy bears and dolls missing an arm or an eye, or wounds drawn on their face with a biro. There were cardboard boxes ranged along every wall, stuffed with rags, offcuts and bits of bedlinen that she'd picked up on her scavenging trips at night, though the boxes soon overflowed and the pieces of ragged cloth and scraps of curtain lying around gradually engulfed everything in sight.

The chairs had been unusable for some time; in fact, they were difficult even to make out, as only two shapeless mounds gave any hint that it had once been possible to sit down in the middle of the room. After a while she and Shuli strung up a line across the room for the latest acquisitions: dried banana peel, because that rattled nicely, bottle gourds, angry looking blowfish, pictures cut out of newspapers and secured with clothes pegs. And they drew: they drew pictures everywhere. On the walls, in the half-used exercise books from the rubbish tips bearing the names of unknown students and with pages that had often turned mildewy after years of mouldering in cellars, only to have Shuli eventually fill them with drawings of palm trees and naked women. Grandma drew laughing faces even around the light switches, and elongated, flowering vines, variegated plants, little monkeys, devils with their tongues sticking out.

The little house stank to high heaven, so generally we would go indoors only to sleep. We tended to live in the garden that ran steep and almost out of sight down the side of the hill. Just don't go out on the highway, she would say, in a leisurely rather than strict tone, as if that were the main source of danger, and with this single warning she considered she'd fulfilled her grandmotherly duties for several days: *'Cause if yer go out, I'll 'ave yer guts fer garters.* What I ate or did during the day, even whether I'd had a wash, didn't seem to bother her at all. As a matter of fact, I'd never seen her having a wash either: she invariably had a bright kerchief knotted under her chin and wore slippers, summer and winter; her ankles were permanently covered in sores and scabs.

I was looking at her feet as she and Shuli dug a ditch in the clay: pale gobs of mud bubbled up between her long, grimy, claw-like toes. Shuli had the kiln up and running in just a couple of days, and after that we were able to fire what they'd made. Can you use it for baking as well? I asked. From this Grandma must have somehow deduced that I was hungry, because she gestured with her chin towards the depths of the garden: *Go and 'ave some almonds. There's brambles, too.*

Her partner Shuli was rarely there. Sometimes he would disappear for weeks on end, always returning with a sack that they sorted crouching by the side of the house. As well as my mother, Grandma had had another child, who had starved to death, or so the relatives said. Long ago, they said, my mother had a little brother, Rudi, who had died of dysentery aged two, because he'd been so hungry that he stuffed himself with unripe apricots.

I never dared ask about it, terrified as I was of the word 'dysentery', and also of Grandma's occasional manic outbursts of fury, when she would flail about with her arms, shouting curses that echoed through the hills: *May they all rot in 'ell.*

Once she disappeared for several days. I thought of my mother, who I hadn't seen for three weeks or more. She'd obviously gone away so she could have her miscarriage in peace and bury the baby quickly, with only her gradually deflating belly as a reminder of the child that had been due. And I thought of my father, who in those days spent his time traipsing around the outer villages with his pop-up shooting range, turning up occasionally with a great deal of hullabaloo, only to disappear as quickly as he'd come.

I sat on the ground in the garden trying, like Grandma and Shuli, to work out the path the ants had taken. The two of them had spent years drawing maps of the army ants carrying their pupae, as if they wanted to tell the future from their black columns in the way that others prognosticated from people's palms or coffee grounds. Then they would use drawing pins to fix the maps to the outside wall of the shed where, though they were to some extent protected by the yellow sheeting projecting from the eaves, they would nonetheless begin to crinkle up and weep coloured stripes from the rain that seeped in.

I sat on the ground, looking at my heels, blackened by the brambles, and had an idea: I'd visit my relatives in Újpest. I knew where they lived, though not how to get there from here. I went down the hill and got a tram, which took me as far as the main square. I knew that from there I had to take a bus, I just didn't know which one. I asked all and sundry how to get to the department store in Újpest, because from there I knew the way to the now-demolished estate, where just a few single-storey houses remained, with the clothes of four or five families drying in the yards of hard-packed earth. Like the others, this was a longish house, with the wreck of a butter-coloured Lada – sans wheels – in the front yard and, on the very last door, a battered sign saying "NO SPITTING." That's where you had to knock. It was late by the time I got there and I was the only one to get off at the last stop. The place was filled with smoke and a dozen or so folk were huddled around the table, which was already laid.

"It's Sanyi's daughter," said a woman who'd fought her way through the chairs and took me to the back. There were men singing loudly; one of them had "ERZSI" tattooed across the back of his hand. Unexpectedly, he looked up at me and roared into the smoke: "Now let's 'ave 'My Dear Old Dad is the Best in the World.'" He burst into song, while the woman held me by the scruff of the neck and steered me into the kitchen at the back, asking: "'ave yer 'ad summat t'eat?"

I gnawed on a drumstick as I listened to the singing. Now and then there'd be an altercation and you'd think they were about to come to blows, but they'd keep on belting out the songs. Meanwhile one of the long-haired women with gold teeth came over and above my head began giving out the plates. "Hey, Ida, look at the head on this kid!"

My scalp had been itchy for several days and when I scratched it large yellowish scales would come off. They left marks where they'd been, like when you graze a knee or an elbow.

While outside the music played on, getting louder and louder, the two women poured hot water into a bowl and washed my hair, and then rubbed something into it that smelled absolutely foul.

It stung my eyes, but in a way it also felt good, as it eased the unbearable itching, which I'd tried to get rid of on my way there on the bus by continually scratching at my scalp with Grandma's gap-toothed comb. Then they made up a bed for me on the cot in the kitchen, and put the door to. From time to time someone would look in and then leave. I was half-asleep and could hear the conversation outside for a long time. "That's not what little Rudi died of. He was just sickly."

Someone told me the story of how Grandma had photographed the dead child on the bier, and to the astonishment of the wailing relatives gathered up her skirts to squat down by the coffin – not to say farewell or to plant a last motherly kiss on the pale little face, but rather to find a more artistic angle to take the picture. Cameras were rare in those days, yet she wouldn't allow hers to be sold off, even after she'd been sacked from every job and had to move out to the little house on the hill. "She always had bats in the belfry," concluded a man with a hoarse voice, "and anyway, sooner or later that Shuli will get it in the neck."

I woke up in the middle of the night with an unbearable itch up my bum. I scratched it but it wasn't blindest bit of use. This went on for several days: I'd be woken by the itch at the crack of dawn, and then lie there in agonies listening to Grandma's snoring until I could snatch another bout of sleep come morning. That's what happened this time, too, and I lay awake for some time in the dark, listening to the snoring from next door and then decided to sneak into the room in the dim light filtering in from the street. Inside it was darker; from behind the blinds came the sound of an early morning bus. I made my way carefully through the randomly scattered items of furniture as far as the sofa with a large, garish picture of the Virgin Mary hanging above it. "Aunt Ida," I whispered into the darkness.

Standing in the kitchen, I had to assume a quite weird position. With my knickers down, I leant forward and clutched my ankles, while my uncle's wife carefully examined my bum in the filthy light of the kitchen lamp. "Fuck the lot of 'em," she said summarily.

She carved a small strip off the carbolic soap with a knife and told me to lie on my front. "It's gonna hurt, but this'll drive them out. It's summat they really hate, this stuff and the garlic." Then she inserted the thin wedge of carbolic, like a suppository, up my bum.

The pain was agonizing, unbearable, pain the like of which I'd perhaps never felt in my life. I sobbed wordlessly as I writhed in the cot, certain I was going to die, that this was indeed death itself, and my insides would all burn and be incinerated, like when someone is struck by lightning, though Shuli always said he wanted to be hit by a bolt from the blue. He'd go out in a storm and stand beneath the almond tree, watching the bolts of lightning, while Grandma would bellow at him from inside the house. It was a little game they played.

By the morning the pain was gone; I just couldn't shit. Auntie Ida wrapped up some meat and potatoes for me, while Uncle Dodó, who had a broken nose because he'd been a boxer in his youth, bent down to me and gave me this piece of advice for the journey: "Tell yer Grandma, she'll get a kick up the cunt. It's a message from Dodó," he added meaningfully, because in Újpest he was used to this statement always adding considerable weight to his words and was quite certain that the macho respect emanating from his bulging, cross-eyed stare was not something that my maternal grandmother – who was in every other respect a born rebel – could fail to be intimdated by, to say nothing of the scrawny, foot-dragging Shuli, who wasn't even a member of the family.

As a matter of fact, we didn't even know his real name: they said he was called Shuli because he was always going on about having completed eight grades of *shuli*, the slang for school, and had his school-leaving certificate. It was never clear what his trade was exactly; at all events, he could draw wonderfully and it was he who taught Grandma how to throw a clay pot, just as she would later explain to me, in due course, how to work the material, to knead the clay so as not to leave any air bubbles in it, otherwise it would explode when it was fired.

It was around midday by the time I got back to the little house. There was no refrigerator, so I left Aunt Ida's box by the wall, in the shade. I thought that since it was covered, it would be safe from the flies.

I gave the clay a little poke, but though it was hot, the pit had completely dried out. I cracked open a few apricot kernels, then, bored of that, too, I went back to the ant map I'd embarked on earlier.

A humid pall of heat descended on the garden, and my skin was slick with sweat, while my hair still reeked of petrol. I lay on the edge of the pit, my head resting on a moth-eaten cushion from the bedroom, and watched the steadily darkening clouds. They towered above us, billowing in a variety of strange shapes, as if the smoke from some forest fire were heading our way from the direction of the valley. The ants were carrying their pupae out, as if they were on to something. There was a kind of implacable determination about this procession. If I put a barrier of little twigs in their way, they would negotiate the obstacle and continue to carry their tiny young to the hidden places they considered safe.

You couldn't tell if it had gone dark because of the dusk that was falling or just the approaching storm; either way, it was getting late by the time I saw Grandma coming up from the bottom of the garden, a carrier bag in one hand and an improbably grey bridal dress draped across her other arm.

"'ad ter go," she said, wheezing. She went into the little house and put down her stuff. An enormous bolt of thunder shook the side of the hill, and the sky was rent by a dry, jagged shaft of lightning. "You eaten?" she said from the kitchen. The paper bags rustled as she took them out of her carrier.

"Ida's sent some grub over."

"Right," said Grandma, without asking who'd brought it, but bent inquisitively over the box I was just opening.

The chipped plate that the meats were on had been completely overrun by ants, just as if I'd poured some poppy seeds over the table. Grandma shook and blew on the unpeeled potatoes several times, while outside the rain began to clatter on the corrugated metal and the tarred sheeting piled on the roof.

"Yer ma's 'ad the child," she said. "A boy."

She managed to more or less shake the ants off one of the drumsticks, and offered it to me.

"But 'e died. Eat up, for 'eaven's sake, or yer'll just waste away."

THE CASTLE

(FRONT LINE)

Every year, in early summer, we would get a visit from Uncle Franci. This year, for some reason, he was late and it was mid-July by the time he rolled up in his battered Mercedes. His black poodle leapt out at once, well ahead of my mother's portly cousin who, his stomach even bigger than last year, could only lever himself out from behind the driving wheel with some difficulty. The dog immediately ran up to my thin teenage legs, rubbing against my socks his pink willie, which came telescoping out, like a lipstick from its case.

"Down, Johnnyboy, get off her!"

Uncle Franci came from Kassa, so he used a diminutive ending whenever he could. *Here, Johnnyboy. Drink up the raspberry juicey, girlie.*

I didn't like the raspberry juicey: the tiny seeds always gathered in the bottom of the glass. That was how it was made by Uncle Franci's mother, who lived in the basement of a house on the bank of the Hernád, in a dim and dark hovel that reeked of cats. Whenever we went to Kassa, we had to go and visit her, to make her day. She would invariably offer us some rather stale pastries on a little plate, and when we said goodbye, she would hold me tight and stroke my head wistfully with her gnarled fingers: *Why don't you stay here with me. I'll get you a piano.*

As always, Uncle Franci came loaded with presents: Bohemian crystal for my mother and, for me, a small china trinket box with a curled-up pussycat on top. He owned an antiques shop in one of the streets off the main square, where his dog lazed all day behind the glass door watching the passers-by. The shop was filled with ticking clocks, figurines and Chinese vases, with silver picture-frames lining the overflowing shelves. He had a number of customers from Hungary, too; he criss-crossed the border regularly, buying and selling *this, that, and the other*, he would say, blinking mysteriously. *Just make sure you don't break anything, Johnnyboy.*

"Right, kids, in we go."

Milena, 25 years his junior, was tall and blonde. In the veins visible through her translucent skin there flowed blood that was neither Hungarian nor Slovak, nor even Jewish. She just about came up to Uncle Franci's shoulders. It was difficult to imagine what she found to like about the old man: in my father's uncharitable words, she obviously thought that he kept cash even under his skin, while my mother said she simply saw him as a father-figure, a claim I must say I found puzzling, as I could detect nothing in the least bit fatherly about this ungainly man with his little explosions of laughter. To my mind, fathers were supposed to be strong and energetic, but above all considerably younger. As for Milena, she was deaf to even the most mildly ironical remark, remaining quiet, gentle and lovely. I adored her clear skin, her shining blonde hair, and the mysterious calm she radiated. She would sit for hours by Uncle Franci's side without saying a word, listening to the Hungarian speech that was virtually unintelligible to her, just taking the occasional sip from her glass and smiling. *Ano, ano*, yes, yes.

I was sorry she hadn't come this time. She had to go to Pozsony for a job interview. Not that she'd get it anyway, said Uncle Franci, with a shake of his head, but let her go by all means, whyever not. The poor dear.

By midday it was dreadfully hot, and the grown-ups were in the front room with the blinds drawn, drinking.

"In you come, girlie. Over here, Johnnyboy, here by my feet. So what were your school reports like? All ones, were they?" he asked, blinking vigorously.

I turned pale, wondering what all this was about, with these ones, but then glancing at my mother I suddenly remembered that Uncle Franci always got the grades the wrong way round, because over in Slovakia, ones are As, not Fs like here, and I began to explain how all my grades were ones. And that I was an outstanding pioneer. Imagine, I said, I got the top pioneer award and I can go to pioneer camp for the holidays, in ten days' time, at the beginning of August.

"Right then, that's good, very good," said Uncle Franci. "Studying's the most important thing. Then you can become a doctor, or whatever for you want."

That's how he always said it, "whatever for you want"; not for the life of him could he learn to say it properly, but apparently even this didn't bother my parents, in the same way that they were willing to overlook some of his other annoying habits, for example that he had a thick, bulbous nose and was constantly snuffling.

"And d'you go them discoteeks?" he asked again. I looked at my mother, as if expecting her to answer, but it was my father who replied: of course she doesn't, that's the last thing she needs in grade seven, to go to the disco.

"And what aboot the lads, then?"

I did in fact have a love, an eighth-grader, who regularly waited for me at the school gate, but I wasn't allowed to get on his Simpson.

I was worried my father might see us, and also a bit scared, so he always rode his motorbike alongside the bus, while I looked out of the window and drew hearts on the glass. Of course, that was none of Uncle Franci's business.

They sent me out to make the coffee, but when they didn't call me in for a long time I sat down in the hallway and just listened to them talking. Earlier, Uncle had told us the story about how this fellow had come into his shop and then kept coming back again and again, more and more often, always knocking something over, and then, imagine, he would just go. But without so much as a by your leave, or whatever for you want, he said, the fellow gave him a glare and left.

I sat outside with the tray, using the sugar tongs to build a tower out of the cubes.

"And then down in the cellar they beat me up. Beat me up so bad that I had blood coming out of my nose, everything covered in blood. Well, I thought to myself, you lot ain't going to scare me. And then I heard our Milena, she was shouting, because they were beating her up bad, too. I ask them, what you doing with my wife. They stare at me, then hit me again, so I thought, well, I got to ask. They couldn't have known, as I did, that she was pregnant, so I say to them, I say, let Milena go, for my sake. Well, they had nothing to say to that, they just upped and went and left me on my own. Quite a bit of time passed and then I heard Milena shouting again, really loud. Then they came back, put a piece of paper in front of me, and said I should sign everything nice and easy, 'cause your dear wife, that's what they said, your dear wife, has told us everything anyway. I signed, and then they let us go home. Well, suddenly, this great feeling of peace came over me, and I knew that they could do what they liked, because this lot, they know nothing. They're bluffing. They made a mistake, you see: if they hadn't said Milena confessed to everything, I might well have believed them. But this way, I realised that this lot didn't know nothing." He shook his head and gave a snuffle. "They didn't know nothing. 'Cause Milena, she would never do such a thing."

The tower collapsed when it reached six cubes high. I took the coffee in.

"Down, Johnnyboy. 'ere you are, but not on the carpet."

I lay on the bed in my room and imagined my beloved being beaten up in a cellar. Then he hears me shouting and, knocking the guards out cold, he bursts in, tries every door in the corridor before finally finding me. He sweeps me up into his lap and together we go out into the light. I am Milena, I have long blonde locks, and I'm sitting behind my beloved on the motorbike. I didn't know whether he could take me going off to camp for two weeks. Whether he'd be faithful for that long, or if he'd find himself another girl, the kind he could take riding up the hill and who didn't have to go home by the time it got dark, who would be allowed to be seen all the way to her front door. I was afraid of August, though Uncle Franci said I should be proud that I was out in front, on the front line, and I was bound to make it as a doctor.

My mother took me to the coach station for the early morning meet-up. We were the first to arrive and hung about in the cool air, a bit at a loss as to what to do, but soon the troop leader arrived and introduced me to the little girl from Tárnok, who was accompanied by her bleary-eyed mother with the thinning hair. Their skin was like parchment. I liked this name, Tárnok: it was an old occupational name meaning "court treasurer", a bit like *titoknok*, the old Hungarian for "secretary": "Mr Tárnok, you have been summoned by His Majesty the King" – and the secretary would hurry to open up the windows of the palace giving out onto the grounds.

There should have been 33 of us in all, but not everyone came to the coach station, because some were being driven down by their parents, even though they had been expressly told not to.

The journey took four hours and nobody wanted to sing. Meanwhile the temperature kept going up, the air was burning hot, and the coach was too heavy to take the wooden bridge from the highway into the village.

At last the castle came into view. It turned out to be neither a fairy-tale castle, nor a lavish newly-built palace, but an extensive block of buildings, with a few two-storey houses and several smaller ones clustered around them. If you didn't know that it was a castle, you'd have thought it was a small town of some sort. From the coach we could see only one tower and you couldn't tell whether it was part of a residential building or of a church. Crows circled above it.

The coach turned off and came to a stop in front of the enormous wrought iron gates. Jagged shadows shimmered in the sweltering heat; it took forever to remove the bags from the belly of the coach. The girl from Tárnok turned away in a bit of a daze and was sick on the gravel. We had to contribute all the food we had brought to the communal store: rolls, foil-wrapped sandwiches, and hard-boiled eggs accumulated on the long, smoothly planed table in the dining hall. Then we piled our bags onto the benches lining the wall, where two people checked there was nothing left in them that might melt or go off, chocolate and that kind of thing. Meanwhile we took our seats at the scrubbed but scratched tables, and waited for our soup. Looking out of the window we could see directly opposite the very tower that rose from the hills in the distance. It turned out to be the tower of a house, perhaps the main building's: it was a charmless, round structure, its bleakness partly disguised by creeping ivy, its tiny windows now blinking as they glinted in the sunlight. There was something deliriously affecting in this: the indistinct, broken-off mouldings on its roof were silhouetted against the blue sky as if drawn there by the hand of a startled or careless child.

The lady in charge of the troop unexpectedly returned: I was horror-struck that she was clutching my red rucksack. She put it down on the bench and when everybody had settled down and all eyes were on her, she took out of it a little round box brown in colour.

"And what might this be?"

My throat was all dry as I answered: it's blusher. My mother got it for me for my birthday. A touch of mountain air, she'd said with a laugh, knowing how bothered I was by the pallor of my skin. The troop leader explained that here we would be out in real fresh air, somewhere that was really healthy, so I wouldn't be needing this, and then she asked if anybody had medicines, cottonwool, vitamins and the like, because those too could be safely left behind, let her not have to say that again.

There were ten of us to a dorm, with the storage cupboards outside in the lobby.

Lights out was at nine. The dusky oblongs of the windows framed the bats flitting about in the park and the dark foliage of the trees swaying to and fro. The alarm went off at six. We had fifteen minutes to get washed, then it was time for morning drill and the raising of the flag. Breakfast was at seven-thirty, after which we went on a goosepimply jog around the castle. The gravel crunched beneath our feet as we did the laps, sweating and shivering.

The biggest problem was having to keep our storage cupboards neat and tidy. In the morning we had to make our beds properly, and then carefully fold and put away our clothes. The bedsheet had to be pulled tight, the pillow plumped up, and the grey blanket laid on the duvet as wrinkle-free as possible. This was the most fiddly part, as the tightly stretched blanket would constantly go saggy, and when it was done, you couldn't sit on it – not that there was any time for that. We would return from our run between eight and quarter past, ready for the distibution of points. Anyone who did settle down on their bed had immediately to hurry and smooth it down, as by the time they entered, the troop leaders had to be met standing to attention. Anyone whose storage cupboard was a mess had all their stuff thrown on the floor and would have to start again with the folding, while the others went off to do some training.

Jutka, who had the bed next to mine and told me in the dark that she lived in Pestimre, was no great shakes at bedmaking.

Once when she was being awarded her points, her answer to a sarcastic question was that "the bedsheet was naturally crinkly." This became a byword in the dorm, every morning all eyes were on Jutka to see how she'd made her bed. On the fifth day she rolled up her bedlinen into a ball, threw it all on the floor, and sobbed that she'd written to her mother asking to be taken home.

Before lunch we stood in a long queue in front of the doctor's office to be given a vitamin C tablet by a sleepy-looking medic in flip-flops. Several of the girls had a crush on him but – though we'd never had a male tutor – I couldn't imagine ever fancying such a pale, blond fellow, whose protruding canines reminded me of my physics teacher. At the end of the first week, the girl from Tárnok disappeared. No one knew where she'd gone: we didn't see anyone come to pick her up, nor did she goodbye to any of us.

In the afternoons, exceptionally, there were no activities scheduled. We went into the village for ice-cream and were shepherded to the gift shop, where everyone could buy something for their parents. Mainly there were picture postcards: a lot of people bought nothing else, but you could also get little wooden pictures to hang on the wall, with a drawing of the castle and the name of the village in curly script burnt into them.

"Don't you like the castle?" asked Miss Ági, to which I shrugged my shoulders to indicate that I didn't have enough money. "Outsiders never like it," she said answering her own question. But then I did in the end pick a postcard, one that showed a green shoreline. Actually, the riverbank looked nothing at all like that, the channel having completely dried out because of the way the water-level was regulated: the strange, mouldering vapour that pervaded the area allegedly rose from the parched riverbed and billowed out along the entire valley. Miss Ági spent the whole time explaining the difference between monocotyledons and dicotyledons, while Jutka went to pick some flowers. As for me, my shoulders ached: I didn't say a word to anyone, even though I'd had a swelling on them for several days, as if I'd been stung by something.

One night one of the girls, a fat and asthmatic seventh grader, wet the bed. It was Jutka who noticed it first. Day was already break-ing and you could hear the dawn chorus; a chill filled the dorm as the steps of the kitchen staff could be heard crunching on the gravel. Jutka woke up the girl, who sat on her bed staring into space, and took a long time to understand that somehow the limp, wet bedsheet had to be got rid of. She stood shivering in her pyjamas while we pulled it out from under her, then Jutka went into the bathroom to rinse it out. The girl meanwhile went back to bed and I promised we wouldn't say anything. We tried to stuff the rinsed bedsheet under her pillow, but it stuck out, so in the end we put it into a bag and simply threw it away. The noise had woken several others, so I looked out to see if there was anyone coming. The doctor was just leaving the terrace of Miss Ági's room: he was wearing just a tee-shirt in the cold air of dawn as he headed for the Castle. Another five days, I thought. Another five years – and then I can get married.

In the afternoon, while we were swimming, I noticed I had a kind of hole in my shoulder. Where before there had been a red swelling, there was now a deep, round hollow, with pus seeping from it. The doctor examined it in some astonishment, put a sticking plaster on it, and gave me another vitamin C tablet. Swimming's out: that does it no good. It will heal in due course, he added, and looked away as if expressing an intense interest in the movement of the wind, for with the afternoon heat, the indefinable but nauseating smell of the channel had intensified.

I hated swimming anyway: we were made to crouch on our towels on the edge of a gigantic concrete swimming pool and at the sound of the whistle everyone had to jump into the water and start splashing around like extras in the poolside scene of some kids' film. I sat in the sun with the hole in my shoulder and thought how already my beloved was on his way to me on his motorbike, he was already here in the village, standing before the wrought iron gates, asking for me by name: but of course, the porter says with a nod, she is in building number III.

By that night I was running a fever. It came with big, soft shadows and deadened noises; I tossed and turned trying to find somewhere cool on the hot bedsheet. Later, as the outlines moved away, I began to get the shivers, so I decided to find the room of the teacher on duty. Everyone was asleep as I made my way barefoot between the beds, the cool of the stone floor feeling really good. The dorm opened onto a narrow corridor: on one side they kept the cleaning stuff, on the other was the door to Miss Ági's room. I knocked, but there was no answer. I waited for a while, unsure what to do, then I pressed down the door handle. First I glanced at the bed, but it was empty. In the half-light I could make out only some rumpled bedclothes and a few items of clothing thrown on the floor. Miss Ági was on the far side, naked and on all fours, her face contorted, and immediately behind her stood the doctor, as if he had let go of her legs right in the middle of pushing her like a wheelbarrow. He slowly turned to look in my direction, and I don't know whether in the gloom he recognised me or not, but either way I had the feeling that for a moment his glance met my feverish and uncomprehending look, and then he slowly turned back, as if he'd just seen a ghost. I closed the door behind me.

I couldn't go back to sleep, my head was throbbing and I felt nauseous. In the morning, in the middle of the run, the world suddenly turned upside down, the sky went askew along with the top of the building opposite. I managed to stagger as far as the stone wall, where I slumped to the ground. The dark shadow on the grass that I'd noticed the previous day turned out to be not a leaf but a dead bat. I picked it up and examined its tiny claws, like those of some prehistoric bird, and the delicate discs of leather on its wings. The folds were velvety soft, friable, like the spores in the cap of a mushroom sliced in two. I put it under a big burdock leaf, then went over to the others who had already run their compulsory laps.

By the afternoon my temperature had soared and I had to be put in the sick bay. When I woke up in the town hospital my first thought was of the little bat. I wondered what had happened to it, whether they had left it in peace under the burdock leaf, or if someone had picked it up as they were raking the grass. I decided that it had been left there, that it had been just sleeping, and when it came to, it returned to the Castle's loft to be with its fellow bats, and in the night it would fly around in the park alongside its bat brothers and sisters.

It was blood poisoning. The nurses came and went, rattling their way along the corridors with their metal trolleys. I was shaken awake at the crack of dawn, and had to clamp a thermometer under my arm. It hurt when they inserted the drip but I felt relieved: surely they wouldn't send me back to the Castle from here. Not tomorrow, not ever. It was now quite certain I was going home.

My parents arrived the next day. My father kept swearing at the stupid teachers and the miserable, dried-up housemothers, while my mother tried to calm him down as we packed up the red rucksack in the small-town hospital.

Afterwards my mother would often say that she was astonished at the sight of my wardrobe: the clothes neatly folded, as if not by any daughter of hers. Her daughter, who always took off her tights and trousers together, who had to have the chewing gum cut out of her hair: yet now, look how she carefully lines up her shoes in the hallway.

My shoulder eventually healed, the miniature crater was replaced by a scab the colour of mother-of-pearl, but I had to wait almost two years for someone in the afternoon half-light of my room to unbutton my blouse and press a comforting kiss on that still-throbbing wound.

Uncle Franci stopped visiting, Mama Vica in the basement of the house on the bank of the Hernád died, the lovely Milena didn't get that job in Pozsony, just as she didn't get a job of any kind, and after her second miscarriage, she was sent to Karlovy Vary, for the waters, to help build up her strength. But she never had any children, and years later another miscarriage convinced her that it was fate, which for some unfathomable reason had decreed that she should spend her life by Uncle Franci's side, accompanying him to the end as a blonde shade, laughing at his jokes and, after his stroke, caring for him with improbable and tight-lipped devotion until his death.

But at that time all this still lay in the distant future. Just a couple of years later Milena was still resplendent in her undiminished beauty as she propelled her long, golden legs from the passenger seat, Uncle Franci clambered out with his usual ponderousness, and Johnnyboy leapt out with the same excitement to embrace the first legs that approached him. This time these legs were bound in gauze, for a scorching hot exhaust pipe can inflict a deep, circular wound on the calves, if you sit carelessly on a Simpson.

"Johnnyboy, you naughty boy, get down! And what on earth did you do to your legs, me angel?"

Milena also directed her gaze at the dressing, and my parents did too, as if noticing it for the first time.

"Oh, that. It's nothing. I took a ride on a bike."

"Well, in you go, my girlie. I've got you some new clothes. And whatever for you want."

TEPID MILK

(BARCODE LINES)

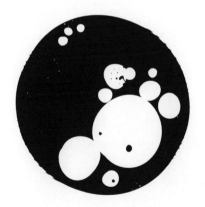

I played out the entire script in my head in advance. It's the kind of thing I liked to do: sketching out scenes and writing up dialogues, leaving nothing to do but wait for reality to play out, as best it could, everything I'd planned. The sequence of scenes in my imagination was generally much more brightly coloured and fast-moving than the actual, real-life film, which consisted of spoken words and movements that chance had interspersed with unnecessary breaks and digressions, sometimes even ruining them entirely.

I'd spent weeks waiting for her. I imagined her arriving in the blinding white of the Hungarian winter, putting down her suitcases and looking around with a broad smile. I repeated to myself the English phrases appropriate for the occasion, to make sure I didn't dry up while performing the role assigned to me. I played out the scene countless times, from various angles, as she entered my room and I showed her the wardrobe I had emptied for her use.

In this mental run-through, her coat was pink. Because her letters were always written on pink notepaper and in the picture of herself that she sent with one of them, she was wearing a pink jumper as she stood in front of a house with a picket fence.

I had only one pink jumper myself, and even that was getting bobbly and beginning to fade from having been washed too often, while its sleeves now barely reached my elbows: my parents had brought it for me from Vienna when I was in eighth grade, and in a couple of years I'd grown almost four inches. As for the light blue slippers that went with it, those no longer fitted at all, but I didn't have the heart to throw them out and kept them in my room, as if I'd just used them, which is to say they became decorative bric-a-brac. Oddly enough, grown-ups felt the same way, treating every object that came from the West with a special reverence; for example, my uncle lined up the empty beercans on top of the kitchen cabinet, as if the massed ranks of the shiny Gössers and Heinekens somehow retained something of the bright lights and excitement of that inaccessible world of women who wore fabulous perfumes and cars that hurtled along broad avenues lined with advertising hoardings. The touchstone of things that came from the West was the barcode: those little black lines imparted a magical allure even to stuff that was otherwise quite ordinary, transforming them into messages from a world beyond our reach, a world of objects in shiny boxes and wrapping paper and people swathed in voluptuous fabrics. No one has ever been able to explain to me the purpose of those little lines and the row of tiny numbers below them. The classmate I regarded as being most in the know, since her parents regularly did their shopping in the special outlets for diplomats out of bounds to ordinary mortals, could say only that the codes were read by a machine at the checkout and told the cashier everything they needed to know. Oddly enough, what that reminded me of was the numbers tattooed on certain inmates' wrists, which made it possible always to identify them by name, age and sex, the only difference being that a barcode betokened not the hell that one heard whispered about within the family, but rather a heaven on earth that was, equally, only whispered about: the world on the other side, where everything was available, where everyone was happy and good-looking and even, to cap it all, unaccountably young. That, at any rate, was how we teenagers imagined it. For if we happened to see particularly good-looking and well-dressed people on the street, the grown-ups would always remark that they must be from the West.

My classmate Robi's bright blue ice-hockey skates, too, came from Vienna, skates which, that season, were to die for at the ice rink. (Later Feri got a pair as well). From then on Robi would go skating every afternoon for a round or two with the envious Czechoslovak boys and the giggly girls with their white skates, who had specially let down their hair.

I too got a new pair of skates from my parents for Christmas. I had great difficulty persuading them not to buy me a pair that I thought too feminine and more suitable for a yummy mummy, and eventually brought them round to what they originally considered too chunky: a pair of black-and-white Alpinas from the second-hand sports goods shop. I didn't want to be feminine: I wanted to be cool. As a matter of fact, the whole point of my going ice-skating was to impress Robi, just as what I had written in biro on my jeans was likewise intended for him, and it was why one afternoon I stood in front of the bathroom mirror having pierced my earlobes. I must have looked quite pathetic with the safety pins dangling from my ravaged ears, but I knew Robi didn't like girls who were too girly and that was why I tried to attract attention to myself in the most outlandish ways I could imagine. Unfortunately I could only go ice-skating on Saturdays; the rest of the time, during our brief conversations in the breaks, I tried to beguile him with black nail-polish and eyeliner that made me look like a panda.

Kathy arrived a good two weeks later than she said she would. She was supposedly visiting relatives near Szeged that she had never met before and who expected her to return after her two-week stay with us, so that they could introduce her to the rest of the family in the village.

What a great time they must have had, we chortled in the corridors, discussing pig-feasts, fisherman's soup, pancakes, Jimmy Carter.

It was not a bright winter's day; it was pouring with rain. The American girl wore a red puffer jacket. Everything she was wearing was red, even her matching wheelie suitcase, while her hair, which in the photos looked to me as if it was brown, seemed to be a dazzling blonde when she took off her knitted cap in the car. I had no opportunity to come out with my practised sentences, for in the pouring rain we had to take everything out of the car quickly, and when we went in I was stunned into silence: my mother didn't make her take off her muddy shoes. Only once before had I witnessed that the house rules didn't apply to everyone without exception: when our class teacher-to-be came to visit us before the start of the school year and my mother ushered her in out of the pouring rain, all laughter and smiles. Kathy did point to her trainers, but my mother shook her head graciously, while I stood shivering in my socks as I waited to hang up her red puffer jacket. So: Kathy was blonde and wore awful braces. My mother was already ladling out the soup by the time I managed to put together a sentence in English and dared ask out loud how long she'd had such light-coloured hair. She didn't understand what I said. She turned her downy, freckle-covered face towards me with an inquisitive smile. I had to repeat the question. She still didn't understand. If at that moment my parents hadn't stiffened up, if I hadn't detected on my father's face every step of his lightning-fast calculations about how much four years of extra English tuition had cost him, if my mother hadn't flashed at my father a flustered 'didn't-I-tell-you-so' smile, then surely I'd have simply pointed to my hair, but in the circumstances I gave up: the colour of her hair was all the same to me and for all I cared she might just as well have been bald.

I concentrated on the pasta swimming around in my soup, wondering whether 'teeth braces' would be in the dictionary. For a little longer Kathy eyed the yellow chicken feet sticking up from the bowl, which my mother had repeatedly asked if she wanted or not, then she put her hands to her cheek to indicate that she wanted to go to bed. As I had embarrassed myself earlier with my question, she no longer turned to me even to interpret and made protesting noises only when I hauled her red suitcase up to her room. That is to say, to my room, which I'd had to clear out the previous day. Kathy looked round appreciatively: at least, my parents gathered from her endless oohs and aahs and thank yous that the place met with her approval. She was still wearing her trainers.

In the morning we were not allowed to make a noise because the American girl was asleep. My mother even asked me to flush the toilet quietly. I said I couldn't do it quietly: either I flushed and then she would be woken up, or I didn't flush at all, in which case around ten o'clock in the empty house she'd be obliged to confront the dreadful truth that in the mornings Hungarians are in the habit of taking a shit. My mother said I was being nasty and vulgar, then asked me if she should make her coffee with milk, to which I answered yes, she should make her one coffee with milk and another one without, and tea as well, just in case, but perhaps we should make a transatlantic call to her parents to inquire what she prefers to drink at breakfast. My mother couldn't take any more of this and shouted at me to get out of the kitchen, how they had made enormous sacrifices to have Kathy over, and that she was, as a matter of fact, my guest, not theirs. I retorted that she was making rather more noise than the flushing of the toilet. And so we arrived at territory that we were both familiar with. From this point on we knew how it would end, with the usual furious exchanges that regularly featured such phrases as *you're an ungrateful wretch, you know we're doing all this for you, you never pay the blindest bit of attention, you live here like a lodger*. I left the house without my school hat and when I was out of sight I immediately rolled down my jeans because on the inside of the turnups were the texts in ballpoint pen to which my mother so strenuously objected. She can't have the foggiest about what's inside, I told myself, not thinking it all the way through, as my mother always turned trousers inside out before putting them in the wash. And that included jeans.

Robi wasn't there for the first class of the day, so it was only in big break that we could talk properly. He was open-mouthed as I held forth on the little monkey in the puffer jacket, painting Kathy as a stupid little rat-face with braces and a whiny voice, topping it off with the detail that she wore glasses.

Each day that week I brought further evidence of the American girl's idiotic behaviour, and after school I had to run home at the double, because she was afraid of our dog, so I had to lock him away, and in the afternoon I always had to take him for his walk. Robi came with me only as far as the tram stop, because he was hurrying to the skating rink, but on the way we both burst out laughing at Kathy's pronunciation of "Duran-Duran", and how lame she looked when bits of salad got stuck in her braces.

Jan-Jan.

No kidding: Jan-Jan.

She doesn't eat meat.

She takes pictures of everything. Even the bus terminal.

In the morning she drinks her milk tepid: we have to take the skin off for her.

And she sleeps with a white teddy!

That last bit I shouted at Robi from the tram, as I watched his back receding into the distance, with the blue skates dangling from his shoulders. What broad shoulders he has.

On Saturday we awoke to a crisp, bright winter's day, just the kind I'd originally scheduled for Kathy's arrival.

My mother asked if I'd be taking the American girl to the skating rink. It's so nice walking through the park.

"She doesn't even have skates," I snapped back.

"Never mind, you can hire some."

My father rushed to my rescue, saying that might be tricky, as he didn't think Kathy would put on skates that had been worn by someone else, but – hang on – let him just dig out from the wardrobe that pair of white ones of his from two years ago, perhaps they would be her size.

"They won't fit," I said.

They did.

Kathy wore a thick white pullover and a white knitted hat, which she took off after her first round and shook out her hair, having quite warmed up. She's doing rather well, I thought to myself. I'd have been happier if she hadn't been, if in fact she'd been barely able to skate at all: it would have been easier for me to point the finger at this girl lurching around on the ice, and to shrug my shoulders: well, what could I do, I had no choice but to bring her with me, like some silly kid brother or sister. Robi bought us some tea, then disappeared into the crowd doing a backwards cross, only to come to a screeching halt behind Kathy thirty seconds later. He repeated this braking manoeuvre a couple of times, then showed her how to move backwards. Kathy fell. He helped her up. He took her hand and led her over to a little group, the in-crowd communing in a little circle.

"I'll get us something to eat," I shouted after them and only when it was my turn in the queue did I realise I had no money on me, having left my purse in my coat in the cloakroom with all the bags.

I was at a bit of a loss. I headed for the loo, but even while I was queueing up I kept an eye out for the blue skates. They were nowhere to be seen.

"Well, what's up? Didn't you get anything?"

They were on the far side of the rink, sitting on a little bench.

"How long are you staying?" Robi asked, and from his careful articulation it was clear that he was asking her for the umpteenth time, but Kathy didn't understand him. At this, with his gloved hand he drew a little round sun in the white dust of the ice, followed by a question mark.

"How many days?" he said in English.

"She's leaving tomorrow," I replied. "So she has to pack this evening." You could have cut the ice with my tone of voice.

Kathy didn't come with me to the cloakroom, but stayed with Robi, and when I got closer to the café, I saw Robi just handing a pen back to the waiter, and then pressing into Kathy's hand a piece of paper, obviously with his address on it. "How many days?" The idiot.

On the bus on the way home we didn't say a word to each other. Kathy dozed off and had to be shaken awake. She went to bed early, taking her white teddy with her.

"She's obviously tired. Did you chat a lot?" asked my mother, who was very pleased with how my English was coming along, and was sure I would learn a great deal more the following week, because that was the secret, the only way, and to cap it all, what a nice and modest girl she was. I wanted to throw up. In the evening I had a go at the black nail varnish but not all of it would come off, traces somehow clinging on near the cuticles, as if I'd been clawing at the earth with my bare hands. Even though I used up half a jar of remover.

The next day Robi was in by a quarter to eight, but didn't say a word to me and went off to the boys' loos for a smoke. Nor did he come over in big break, or during the double history class that followed, where the teacher never had a break anyway, so I knew we wouldn't be able to talk at all that day.

This woman, by the way, happened to be our class teacher. She was a big, dumpy, motherly type, in her forties, in whose broad, dull face only the unusually widely spaced teeth offered anything of even passing interest. She seemed awfully old and spoke extremely slowly, without expression or pause, summarising what she said earlier in fatuous bullet-points. She was initially keen to win us over, but we felt that her no doubt well-intentioned efforts were, in fact, rather strained. And I also hated the way she sat on the front bench with her feet propped up against the back of the desk. Today she'd happened to forget the textbook, so she asked for mine, as I was the one sitting nearest to her. She wore opaque knitted tights, which made her calves bulge out even more, and the hairs on her legs penetrated even the thick brown material. She might at least have shaved her legs. Even I did, though mine were nowhere near as hairy. I was just musing on this when I suddenly remembered the sentences I'd inscribed in my copy of the textbook.

I often wrote very personal messages in the bottom margins. I drew the letters extra long, so they became distorted and stick-like, which made the written words look like parallel stripes. And when I also made the stem of the letters a little thicker, the secret message looked like a barcode: to decipher it you had to look at it from a different angle. If you tipped the book to one side, and held it in a way you never would when reading, it was possible to make out the writing thanks to the foreshortened angle. It took a long time and a great deal of effort to produce these kinds of letters, and sometimes I got so engrossed in drawing the lines that I wouldn't notice if someone was calling out to me.

This time, too, class was a dreadful drag, and only once did I manage to come to, on hearing the word 'luddite': she seemed to be summing up, I thought. The next time I surfaced, I could sense that something was up. The class was paying close attention as the teacher held my book flat, almost horizontal, before her eyes.

"Well, now. That's interesting."

She turned the book this way and that, her eyes narrowing.

The class was all eyes and ears and she must have felt that she couldn't miss this unexpected opportunity to cross the invisible line that she must have suspected – rightly – a teacher ought never to cross, but if that was the price to pay for revelling in the unprecedented feeling of being complicit with her pupils, then so be it: she was prepared to sacrifice one soul for the sympathy of the other 28. She didn't for a moment glance in my direction: that was part of the game.

"Well, now. That's interesting," she repeated. "I can see something written here."

Short pause for effect.

This was the point of no return. She held the book at an angle and began to read out the words.

I knew what was coming. It was open at the timetable page.

''I love you, my sweetest Robi."

I sat motionless, holding my breath, not daring take out a tissue in case the resultant stirring of the air drew attention to my devastated and defenceless body. Though I sat there, I felt I was a puppet, an extra rehearsing for a role in her own life, someone for whom this time the negative form of the regularly repeated statement at roll-call was entirely appropriate: Not present. The class didn't burst into laughter, playing no part in the game, but sat in silence, as when waiting for their marked work to be handed out.

When the bell went I was finally able to inhale. Until then it seemed that the foul vapours choking my chest were also fogging up my brain, slowing down my pulse thanks to a welter of harrowing, unrelenting images. I imagined her with her face disfigured, sick, in a wheelchair, but my frenzied imagination was unable to conjure up the only scenario that might have offered some relief, the one in which the roles assigned to us would have been reversed.

The teacher, who wouldn't normally have held a break at this point in class, heaved herself up from the bench, and flung my book casually back where the exercise book was.

"I must just run down to the common room for a moment. Stay here all of you, I'll be back in a minute."

I had to take a quick decision, so lightning fast that I couldn't think my plan all the way through.

In the corridor I called out after her.

"Miss! ... I must ... have a word ... with Miss."

She turned round, her face impassive, only in her eyes, in her almost blind, little grey eyes, did there lurk some unidentifiable gleam that resembled, if anything, Schadenfreude.

"Is it urgent? Can't it wait?"

I couldn't allow myself any display of emotion, as everything depended on being able to strike the right note, the note that would now stop her in her tracks. I couldn't afford to appear either too agitated or too intimidating.

"My parents ... will be coming ... to have a word with Miss ... about the hospital..."

This caught her off guard. She was expecting something else. Bingo. I got into my stride.

"I ... wanted to ... tell Miss ... that the test results ... have come."

Several heads popped round the classroom door and saw us facing each other in the corridor. She found this embarrassing, as it must have looked as though I was taking her to task for what had happened.

"Come down to the common room," she said.

Sentences began to form in my head– great, charismatic actors know the feeling – but on the stairs I unexpectedly stumbled and began to sweat as I flushed.

We sat down in the corner of the common room set aside for smokers. She turned to face me with reluctance and no more than dutiful curiosity, and I saw she kept glancing at her watch.

I began as if I'd been entrusted with a non-commital, official message which it was now time to communicate. Neither my tone of voice nor my face betrayed any emotion. I also knew I mustn't be long-winded, as too much detail could lead to questions, and questions, even in the short term, were dangerous, for I suspected that in any case many hours of suffering lay ahead before I could have my vengeance for that single, irrevocable minute.

"These days ... I am ... so dreadfully tired," I said, making it sound like a confession. "I'm sure ... Miss ... has noticed."

"So?"

"And so my parents took me to see a doctor ... so ... it seems ... we've just got the results ... and it's turned out ... that..." Here I paused briefly for effect. "It turns out I have leukemia."

The teacher's face turned pale with terror. Making the most of her paralysed silence I added that I was very likely facing a long period of hospital treatment, that as a matter of fact I wasn't feeling that good just now, and that actually my parents hadn't wanted to let me go to school this week, because I needed a lot of rest before starting treatment and had to take a lot of vitamins, but I wanted to come, Miss knew why, and I gave her a meaningful look, so, anyway, I would be absent for a while and I would miss her, too, but ... I was on a roll. I'd have liked to add something about the consequences if I happened to die, but with an instinctive sense of proportion I allowed myself only to hint that this was certainly a possible outcome, though quite a likely one. Meanwhile I was indeed sweating profusely, and even my eyes began to fill with tears for some reason, which is, of course, an obvious symptom of pneumonia. As we had never before had an opportunity for such a personal, one might even say intimate, conversation, and in the close on two years we had known each other she'd never had any reason to cast doubt on anything I'd said, she was incapable of responding with anything sensible. In her gaze, which she intended to be sympathetic, there was a kind of resentful impatience, as if her eyes were saying: this was the last thing I needed.

"Wouldn't you ... like to ... go home?" she asked, in a quite different tone of voice.

I sat immobile, like someone without the strength even to stand up, who had, in these last few hours, used up her final reserves of energy.

She asked if I wanted someone to go with me, and promised to speak as soon as possible with my parents, while assuring me that I shouldn't worry about missing class, and said several times that I shouldn't now concern myself with anything but my health. Indeed, she got so much into the swing of things that she grasped my hand like a doctor trying to infuse courage into their patient through their hands. This suddenly struck her as embarrassing, and she stood up.

The bell had long gone by the time we headed back to class. As I packed my bag, I could feel the others' confused and uncomprehending stares like daggers in my back. The teacher began class, and as I left the classroom, I took a long, perhaps final look at them all through eyes brimming with ill-health, and said goodbye to her with a meaningful look.

"Take care," she said as I closed the door behind me. I was truly dragging myself along as if I lacked the strength to take a single step.

I went down to the basement, straight to the lockers. Robi's was at the far end: he kept his skates and hockey stick in the corner, between his metal locker and the wall, as there was no room for them anywhere else. His locker was crammed full of all kinds of junk, some records and an anorak on the shelf, gym things underneath. I put on my coat and hat, and then my gloves. I flung the skates over my shoulder and grabbed the hockey stick. I left through the back gate, worried that if I used the main entrance she might see me from the classroom. She rarely walked up and down during class, but now I was afraid she might look out and see me.

To be on the safe side, I hauled myself as far as the tram stop, but once on the tram, I rested the hockey stick against me like some kind of lance. The two skates were tied together by their laces, which it took me nearly until we got to the Körtér to undo; I even managed to break a fingernail. Why so damned tight, you dummy. The idea that the passengers assumed I was on my way to the skating rink appealed to me. A fragile girl with leukemia and ice hockey gear.

I threw one of the skates into the metal litter bin on Villányi Street, the other I carried to the end of Karinthy Frigyes Street and chucked into a wheelie bin there. I couldn't have broken the stick in two, so I left it propped up in a doorway: someone might be able to make use of it.

I was hoping that Kathy wouldn't be in. I'd have liked never to see her again, to have had her secretly taken away at daybreak, like our old dog, without having to say goodbye, so I'd never have to hear another word about her, so I could expunge her from my memory as if she'd never existed.

As I opened the garden gate, I sensed she wasn't there. The dog's bark was somehow different. Wagging its tail furiously, it ran joyously to the fence: it wanted its walk.

I went over, as if to let him out, then at the last moment I shut the little gate again and turned my back on him. I saw that his water was frozen solid. He threw himself against the metal mesh, barking wildly: he thought this was a new game of some kind. When I closed the entrance door behind me he realised he'd been misled, that for some reason we weren't going for a walk and he would remain shut into his two by two metre pen.

I heated up my lunch, put it on a plate, then poured it all down the loo, leaving the plate and the fork in the sink. I threw a scrunched up napkin after them.

I lay down on the couch fully dressed and tried to concentrate. I concentrated as cell by cell, drop by drop, my blood turned white, because that's what I imagined leukemia was like, a feeling as if you turned pale from the inside, little by little, insidiously, irreversibly.

I could hear from outside the dog's bursts of high-pitched yelping and the clinking of his water dish as he pushed it to and fro. I thought that if I now cut open my veins, a thick, white liquid would come oozing ever so slowly from my wrists, down onto the carpet, congealing as a film formed on top of it, like on tepid milk.

BLACK
SNOWMAN

(GRID LINES)

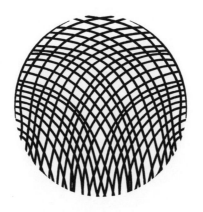

A copybook with boxes was was not, as a matter of fact, full of boxes, since boxes, as obviously everyone knew, even in class 2/A, are three-dimensional, though for some reason Miss still called it a copybook with boxes, even though she invariably corrected the children when they called it that. And she corrected even their parents, who had to buy them and were just as confused, but simply accepted the situation. They needed to buy copybooks with boxes, and that was that. Two just ruled, one with boxes. And so parental brains would be completely befuddled and ask for a copybook with boxes, to which the shop assistant responded by saying there was no such thing.

"Are you sure you don't mean a copybook with grid lines?" she asked.

"Yes, that's right, with boxes, quite large format," the parents would nod in a daze: to them it really was all the same. The stationer's was in a wooden hut in the middle of the estate, with small concrete slabs across the grass down to its entrance, but the grass had been rapidly worn down even where it had managed to grow.

All around it, as far as the eye could see, stretched blocks of flats ten storeys high. To the right glowed the red buildings of the kindergarten, with their illuminated side-panels: I could have made it that far, but as for getting home, I was less sure. From a distance, the blocks looked absolutely identical and the reference points (corner shop, grocer's, litter bin perched on a telegraph pole, graffiti) were only visible if you went the usual way.

The overall scene, though, was reassuring and familiar as far as I was concerned. This was the landscape I had seen ever since I was a child, endless grid lines in every direction, with lit-up windows that to me meant reassurance and order. Those moving into the flats invariably encountered wall-to-wall grey bouclé carpeting, windows with faux-silk curtains of spinach-green, and patterned lino in the hallways, the kitchens and the bathrooms. And in the children's rooms mass-produced kids' wardrobes: every family was asked where the youngsters would be put and that was where they set up the kids' red, green and yellow building-block-like furniture. My parents opted for the room which had a balcony, but on the third floor, at the Fintas, the endlessly bickering kids ended up on the far side, in the smaller room, as they did at the Ledneczkis on the ground floor: only later, after the birth of baby Öcsi, did they move their daughter over to the other side. On the tenth floor, too, at the Jakabs, the back room became the kids' room: one bank holiday they managed to set fire to our balcony while the boys were surreptitiously playing with fireworks and a spark that landed on the seventh floor ignited a petrol canister made of plastic. I woke up amid the flames in a room bustling with people, mainly neighbours, shouting at each other: the whole thing had something of the excitement of a film about it, and a few days later by the sooty black wall of the balcony I found a dish of aspic with a pig's snout in it pointing skywards. I ran screaming to my mother: this animal, part-preserved in aspic, is forever bound up in my mind with the terrifying memory of the flames.

Down at the Ledneczkis', too, they once had a fire. Little Öcsi, as he was always known, was constantly ill and on one occasion was down with an inflammation of the middle ear. This was being treated with an electric heater when the teddy bear propped up against it caught fire. There, too, it was the small room with the balcony that burnt out, and although they too managed to quickly put out the flames, the story continued to circulate amidst the tower blocks for many weeks, like the smell of the smoke: "the teddy caught fire", and "the curtains were ablaze in seconds", sentences like those did the rounds of the estate. Thus did two soot-blackened rooms on Staircase 7 become lodged in the mythology of the estate, much like the little boy's beheading, another story we heard in a hundred different versions when we moved in: he got stuck in the lift, looked out of the lift window on the seventh floor (oral tradition varied as regards the actual scene, but it was most often on the seventh floor, seven being a magic number) and whack, the lift sliced his head off. And then there was also the story of the girl who fell out of the seventh-floor window – that, too, everyone had heard about, though no one seemed to have known her in person.

Have you heard? The mothers asked one another as they shook their heads in front of the laundrette or the ABC, the state food store, both of them in the square between the blocks of houses, in an aluminium building with corrugated walls. Have you heard? And the lady in the laundrette would nod, yes, she'd heard and then hand out the towels which were, of course, yet again someone else's: sighs, clattering, rummaging about, and I trudged home alongside my mother, who was carrying the sports bag, and the very next time I had a go at sticking my head out of the lift window trying to imagine how the lift could have sliced off the little boy's head, but I couldn't get it to open, and anyway it wouldn't have been big enough to get a normal head through: he must have been a boy with very small head. This window, by the way, as I remember it, fulfilled no function at all, no one could ever want to look in or out of the metal door covered in graffiti; only the tenants would tap on the frosted glass in the mornings, to indicate their impatience ('What's up?') if the lift took too long at one of the floors.

There was constant tapping on the pipes, too. The house was filled with mysterious noises: empty bottles and potato peel echoed as they clattered down the rubbish chutes, water would come cascading down, radios boomed, the Szabó girls on the first floor dashed around in their noisy clogs, to which the Geres below them, the janitor and his family, responded by banging on the ceiling with broom handles.

Concierge, that's what was written on their door, and it was really strictly forbidden to call old Gere the janitor. Mrs Gere planted marigolds in her window boxes, old Gere did the cleaning, and his mother sat all day long on a stool by the back door, telling her beads. They didn't use the laundrette opposite: old Mrs Gere spoke with the utmost scorn about 'women today', who wouldn't do their washing themselves, and insisted on doing her own starching, as well as hanging out her washing herself, while her husband washed down the Lada every Saturday, going over to the café afterwards, saying *what's up, Ma?* as he passed by his mother's flat on his way home: *so what's up, Ma?*

The café was opposite the entrance to the ABC, a little beyond the same aluminium building that housed the laundrette. This is where they sold soft ices, half a forint a scoop. If we wanted one, we would buzz mum on the entryphone and she would lean out of the window and drop the coins wrapped in a piece of paper. Otherwise it was the back of the building that the mothers leaned out of, as that was the side the playground was located, in order to keep an eye on their kids, who would be chasing each other around the concrete table tennis table, or roller skating, or cycling around the block.

The Dékány kids had to go in when the cushion made an appearance in the window. The family had a fancy, orange-coloured cushion that they'd put in one of the third-floor windows when dinner was ready. You could work out from the lights on the staircase roughly what time it was. When my father came home, the light went on in the living room, whereas until then it was on only on the other side of the flat, in the kitchen. I was allowed to stay out until the streetlights came on, and as for the Ledneczki kids they just got a shout from the ground-floor window, which they invariably failed to hear, so that a few minutes later their mother would shuffle out in her slippers to say "the feature's about to start." As a matter of fact they were never able to watch the film without being interrupted, because the postboxes were right by their living room and those coming home late would always bang their boxes' aluminium flaps when picking up their post. Another thing making life hard for them was the heavy door of the glass-covered bicycle shed, which invariably thudded shut with a frightful bang. That was another reason they were always saying they would move; at least, that's what they'd been saying for all the fifteen years I had known them to live there.

As for the Jakabs on the tenth floor, what they suffered from was the lift-shaft. It was like living next to a gigantic, irregularly beating heart: they could hear day and night the wheezing and humming soul of this gigantic concrete creature. Inside the lift-shaft, as if in some vertical tunnel in hell, hung veins of rubber cording and cables as thick as a human arm connected to springs that came and went who knows where. In the innards of the rubbish chute, despite old Gere's best efforts to hose out the wheelie bins, big fat slugs settled every summer, and Kovács and his kid brother had to use their fingers to winkle them out in order to stuff them in jamjars for fishing bait.

Whenever the lift was out of order we had to queue at one of the other staircases at the far end of the building. If this happened, someone in that block would have to let us in and when we got to the tenth floor, we'd file across the upper fire corridor to our own staircase. The top floor was steeped in the smell of hot tar, fat pipes swathed in asbestos ran the length of the walls, and by the exits to the roof there hung a red skull on a metal plate by way of warning.

Though we once managed to get out onto the roof, not even the most daring of us risked going all the way to the edge. The entire length of the building was lined with individual little houses covered in metal, like houses for living in, but of mysterious use. On the tar sheeting the water stood in little pools, while the entire roof was covered with tiny pebbles, and along the length of the wall, like some loose lock of hair, the big flap of a rubber gasket waved in the wind. We had the halfwit with us as well. He was someone we were all scared of; we didn't even know his name, only that he lived on the fifth and that his mother was quite old. The halfwit must have been about our age, but quite a lot taller: he was in short trousers and blew gobs of snot and saliva in the lift, and now, squealing in a joyous but unpleasant voice, flapped round and round the roof on his thin, flamingo-like legs. We stood among the aerials with pounding hearts, in the gusty wind. To the right you could see the still-pristine wheatfields, with the green patch of the Kiserdő's trees, while on the left sprouted an endless forest of houses, the tram terminus, the red and blue of the kindergarten, the stationer's, and the grid lines of the housing estate with its bright balconies and windows: our home.

The Kiserdő suicide was one everyone had heard of. There was once a man who left the grid lines, trotting off the page, beyond the margins, down all the way to the Kiserdő. By the time they found him, his feet had reached the ground ... said the laundrette lady, lowering her voice to a whisper, and of course this was something else I couldn't understand, just as I couldn't the beheaded boy: I wasn't clear how someone who had died could continue to grow, and why they didn't find him sooner, as the Kiserdő had so many visitors.

On occasion we too would dare to venture that far on our bikes; in fact, we sometimes went all the way to the quarry, but that was here-be-dragons country, with scary laws of its own that we didn't know about, and full of rough tracks going off in various directions. Our world really consisted of the oblong in front of and behind the four blocks; this was where everything of importance in our lives took place.

It was here that Laci pocketed the first of his teeth that had fallen out once when he went cycling, it was here that we sat on the grass during hot summers on outspread blankets discussing who was in love with who (which staircase did they live on?), it was here that we left each other messages in chalk on the concrete, the letters as big as possible, so they could be read even from the upper floors.

I was terribly pleased when the boys began to make presents to the girls of my oak apple necklaces. The oak apples, which I collected from the Kiserdő, I first shaped into rough cubes on the concrete before decorating them. Soon all the kids on the staircase were wearing them, strung along leather thongs that hung from their necks alongside their latchkeys.

In those days the area was overrun by giant cranes, as the housing estate was expanding. Gigantic trenches were being dug, lit by blue-tinged floodlights at night, with heavy lorries coming in long convoys to fill the ditches. Hills and valleys emerged from the ground, the work of Creation was continuing apace, privet hedges and little trees with delicate trunks supported by rods appeared along the pavement edges. A bigger ABC opened, their state-of-the-art conveyor-belts at the checkouts even made it onto the TV news: no more long and tiring queues, we heard on the TV, so we went and joined the queue. Enormous planters had been placed in front of the "big" ABC. In those days the balconies didn't really have much in the way of flowers, as people used them for storing boxes and tools, cupboards that didn't fit indoors, and mattresses for their weekend huts, so these islands of flowers brightened up what was otherwise a vast sea of concrete.

When we were studying petunias in grade five, everyone had to bring one to biology class. My mother learnt on the phone from the Végváris that there was a whole bunch of them in front of the big ABC and that they'd already picked some. It was evening and my mother didn't feel like walking over there so late, so we only stopped there the next day on the way to school in our little Polski Fiat. The one thing she forgot was that, because of the integrated national syllabus, every fifth-grade class in every school for the hundred-thousand-strong populace of the housing estate would be studying petunias, so that by the morning all we found was a row of empty stone planters, stripped of all their ornamental flowers. Végvári and I shared a petunia as we bent over the microscope: look, children, how there's a sugary liquid in the stem and, sure enough, ever since then I've been fond of petunias.

In the area between the playground and the three-storey-high buildings there suddenly appeared what was later to become the sledding hill. It was from here that the Jakabs brought some strange, curiously light, sponge-like stones gleaming with an oily sheen that reflected all the colours of the rainbow, of which they said there were many more, and out of which I carved my first successful work of art after the oak apple cubes, namely the black snowman. That snowman became Szilvi's, while I perfected my technique a small step at a time, making use of even my mother's nailfile to create increasingly sophisticated objects out of the relatively soft, crumbly material. I made a ring for Tibi Laczkó's pregnant wife, who was always sunbathing and who invariably smiled as she admired the fascinating little ornament on her finger. Then I made toy furniture, a few bangles – though these immediately fell apart – and, finally, pearls by the dozen. After a while all the little girls in the neighbourhood were wearing my necklaces, and brought in exchange sachets and little boxes with Barbie-doll shoes, stickers and decals, anything that might possibly be bartered for the ornaments. Creation was continuing to press on at a feverish pace, as the soil filled with thousands of twisting pipes, cables, and layer after layer of dirt, and the pearls proliferated, as did the treasures in my caskets that I got in return.

That mysterious, sponge-like stone that glittered in oily colours, the like of which I have never seen since, that mineral with the magical sheen of which the sledding hill was made and of which there was by now a little piece in every flat, that substance was – I now know – an extremely dangerous waste by-product: blast furnace slag full of heavy metals, tar, and slow-degrading toxins that gradually filled the earth and the trunks of the trees, seeping ever deeper down beyond the lift-shafts, into that cable-swathed hell, as the mica hung in the air we breathed and settled in our lungs and was carried gently by the wind right up to the tops of the ten-storey blocks, beyond the uppermost lines inscribed with wispy clouds, and higher still, up to where, according to Ma Gere, there lay the Kingdom of Heaven.

INSULATED FLOOR

(TRANSPORT LINE TICKETS)

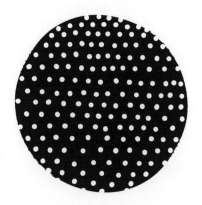

"You Fradi or Dózsa?" asked Big Tibi when I stopped in the doorway. I knew what I was supposed to say, I just didn't understand why we had to play this silly game of 'City or United?' every time. Though I must say, I did like the way he hoisted me up and said "Hey, come on, what you waiting for?" Once I'd given the only possible answer – Fradi –, Big Tibi would ceremonially lift me high into the air, spin me round, then delicately nudge me into the room: "You're a softie, my dear. Dózsa fans can't even cross the threshold," he would declare, every time, for the benefit of the nonexistent audience out in the corridor, before he closed the door: "just so as you know."

Little Tibi, who was my schoolmate but in the B-stream and eighth grade, had recently got a room of his own. Actually, it wasn't a proper room: they had turned the area above the kitchen into a mezzanine, with the upper part of the kitchen window providing natural light and ventilation for the space above, where you couldn't really stand up straight, though you could hide there rather well. When he was in his parents' bad books, his father simply took the ladder away and he had to suffer the kitchen smells in silence until Auntie Vica let him come down when the door had slammed shut behind his father. Once he left you knew he wouldn't be back anytime soon, and in the evenings they preferred to be in bed by the time he came home because then he found it more difficult to pick a fight with them. In fact, or so Little Tibi said in the school-yard during big break, even Auntie Vica apparently slept up there the other day, taking her sequined duvet and pulling the ladder up after herself.

His father was inordinately proud of the mezzanine he had built above the kitchen, and adopted a strident tone when showing visitors the wall of chipboard plastered with newspapers, winking knowingly as he commented on the pictures of naked women that his son had pinned to it.

And indeed, Little Tibi was always after my pin-up calendars. It was the 3D calendars that were most highly prized in class: you could get two or three ordinary ones for a 3D one, but he wasn't interested in those with iridescent cars or ships, only the Skála store pin-up in thigh-high boots. Pointing to a Boney M. poster he asked me if I knew what a black pussy was like and whether they were also black down there. And he added that, according to his father, blacks had big cocks, so the girls, too, had to be big *down there* because that was surely the only way a black chick could make babies with a black guy. As for me, I had been avidly collecting transport tickets for the past year, but he didn't have the slightest interest in those. I kept them in a box: I even had a ticket from the Paris metro, and one of my mother's colleagues brought me a genuine one from America, with a red stripe.

It all began when Laci Vida claimed he had an example of every single kind of ticket. He had every possible pattern that the conduc-tors punched in when validating a ticket, so to get a free ride all he had to do was pick the appropriate one if an inspector came. Unfortunately, not once since he had completed his collection had an inspector come, and previously when caught out he had always given a false address, or at least so he said. Though I had a season ticket, I was so impressed that I also began collecting regular tickets, then I somehow kept getting more and more from acquaintances as well. I loved to open the box and sort the colourful pieces of paper. Later I repurposed a plastic folder and sewed little pockets for each of the various kinds of ticket, and below each one stuck a little label with the name of the country on it. Little Tibi asked why I didn't write the country name on the ticket itself. Such a barbaric thought had never crossed my mind, and I could see that he was only asking in order to pass the time, but I promised that next time I'd also bring the new ones from abroad to show him. I even had a Romanian return ticket that had to be punched at both ends, once on the way there and once on the way back. It looked like a yellow domino. That was my favourite at the time.

The following week I went over with my parents, because they wanted to discuss putting down floor insulation, as there was a special offer on. Auntie Vica's brother had had it laid two years earlier in her flat on the estate nearby. This spurred Big Tibi to put down the red lino by himself, working with his son. He thought the kid was all right and quite handy, you just had to push him a bit.

We sat up in the mezzanine, amid the smell of vanilla, tucking into the freshly baked rolls, though it was strictly forbidden to take food up there. I found Little Tibi's half-hearted browsing of my prize collection irritating, as he kept running his nails along the edge of the plastic folder. He was trying to get me to have a smooch again and to show him *down there*, we were bound to hear if someone was coming anyway. And he claimed he knew I'd let Roland see it, but that wasn't true.

"Well, all right then," I said and, offended, I let myself down the ladder. I puttered about in the kitchen, looking at the red pots and the covers with red hearts that Auntie Vica had sewn for the chairs. In the lounge the grown-ups were just drinking some Hubertus and playing roulette. I liked the roulette-wheel and watching the ball spinning round and round, and the way they piled up the colourful chips. There was little else to play with here: one of those push-down ashtrays with a spring under its metal top which took the cigarette butts down into its dark, foul-smelling belly, and a plastic manikin pis figure you had to pour water into the head of and then you pulled its trousers down to make him pee, but we thought this was rather lame. Big Tibi, though, took a childish delight in it, guffawing loudly as he told my father how last time Little Tibi, too, almost wet himself, though he barely raised a hand to him, but still, no matter, the main thing was that a child should fear his father. Auntie Vica pointedly began to offer us cake and my father looked at me and asked: and by the way, where would Little Tibi be?

Because I should let him know we have a job next week. And there'd also be something for me to do. At weekends my parents always went to their country cottage, so it was particularly fortunate that I wouldn't be at home by myself and could eat at Auntie Vica's.

As they laid the carpet I preferred to just watch. It was fun to see them hauling in the huge roll and then spreading it out. It was like a whale. We visited all kinds of interesting flats: there was one with a parrot that managed to bite my finger, another where they'd locked the dog out on the balcony, where it howled all the time we were there. Big Tibi trimmed the edge of the carpet with a stanley knife, then glued a grey plastic strip all around the walls that had to be held there for a while to make sure it stuck firm. It was mostly grey or moss-green bouclé that we laid down, those were the most popular colours at the time. Big Tibi invariably had a few words of praise for the flat and the view, while telling Little Tibi off, which was somehow part of the job, like the beer and the thank you so much and goodbye.

"You have a great view from here. These flats are rather good, central heating and everything. Because wherever you are, you have to do the same blessed thing." We always ended up with that as he concentrated on using the stanley knife, and somehow he always got round to his mantra about *that lot*.

Laying down lino was much more exciting. His father cut the pieces to size while Little Tibi laid a serrated metal sheet on the floor and the back of the lino and waited for the lumpy glue to dry. I loved this smell: it was both heady and headache-inducing at the same time, like the smell of petrol or shoe-polish. When they smoothed down the part that was ready, it was my job to rub the whole lot down with a brush and smooth the air bubbles out, pushing towards the edges. This was not easy to do, as there would alway be a trail of bubbles and even when the surface seemed to be level, if you looked at it from the side, the odd sneaky little peak or two would always pop up. What I'd have liked to do most of all was the cutting, as I loved the thin curly strips trimmed from the edges, but even Little Tibi wasn't allowed to do that, only his father. He worked half lying down, propped up on an elbow, and the attention he had to pay made him build up quite a lather. Dammit, he kept saying, and groaned a lot, damn and sod and blast the bloody thing.

A more complicated floorplan, say an entrance hall or a bathroom, where you also had to go round built-in cupboards: well, that took up to ten bottles of beer. In these cases Big Tibi first made a paper pattern, turned it round and drew its lines along the back of the lino, then took great care as he cut round it. Meanwhile of course his throat was inevitably parched and either he would send me out for more beer, or went off to fetch some himself – which is just what he did on that particular Saturday, towards the tail-end of autumn.

We'd been at it since the morning and had only just finished our packed lunch when we started on the lino in the hallway. In the inside rooms the carpet was all laid, and we had carried the offcuts out to the refuse chute. Big Tibi made the paper pattern while – unusually for him – praising his son. He was on a high; we were making good money. You don't really have two left hands, he said, giving the lad a dig in the back, then allowed him to cut the paper pattern himself with a pair of scissors. When this was successfully accomplished, Big Tibi let us take a break and we hunkered down by the wall on the newly-laid carpet with its intense fabric-y smell. We were doing well for time: the owners weren't coming back until the following evening. We started horsing around. Little Tibi was trying to scare me with a strip of grey plastic –snake! snake! – and pretended that the snake was trying to get into my knickers, while Big Tibi was laughing his head off. I think he must have had quite a lot to drink, as it was unusual for him to let us twist his cauli-flower ears, while he whinneyed as we tickled him. Way back he had been a coach for Fradi, only he had to leave for some reason that he never mentioned. Now that I leaned so close, I could see how frightening his squashed, battered nose was, with those two dead eyes on either side of it. We got so carried away that in the end Little Tibi and I were rolling from one side of the room to the other, and his father was determined to sing come what may, though we didn't know any of the songs he launched into in his hoarse voice. And I was really surprised when out of the blue Little Tibi told his father the story about the bus conductor that I'd already heard in school on Friday. I don't think even Auntie Vica knew it, but now, in this unusual and light-headed atmosphere of intimacy, he somehow felt the need to share something with his father, so that beyond the careful but monotonous movements of their labours, they could bond over some male secret. Little Tibi knew Laci Vida's story about the inspector and now proceeded to present in colourful, almost boastful detail how he too once gave a false address on the bus, how he wrested his arm free of the grip of that cretin of an inspector, and how he fobbed them off with an address in Rákos where we had recently done a job.

"'Cos they sure aren't going to mess around with me," he insisted, casting a sidelong glance at his father. Big Tibi said nothing: it was impossible to tell what was going on in his head. At all events, the appreciation that Little Tibi was fishing for failed to materialise, and his father began to put his tools away and fold up one after the other the paper templates that were now all over the place. I felt relieved when he finally said something:

"You can finish it off by yourselves. I'm going out for a walk and to get some ciggies."

We worked fully aware of the weight of adult responsibility on our shoulders. While Little Tibi held down the template I drew the line. It seemed to be accurate. We heaved sighs of relief and began cutting from both ends.

"Hey, stop jiggling it about," he said, so I did and let him come all the way round to me with the stanley knife. We sheared off the edges and raised the pattern we had cut out. It was an exciting moment.

As Little Tibi stood there, red in the cheek, holding up the cut out piece, suddenly a kind of panicky suspicion crossed my mind, but when he once again laid the material down along the floor, we gasped with horror. We looked at the floor and neither of us could speak. He was the first to be able to say something:

"Fucking hell. He's going to kill us. Fucking hell."

We hadn't turned the pattern round, so we had cut all of the hallway lino in reverse: with the reddish surface facing downwards it fitted to a T. It was the ugly, greenish-grey plastic underside that was up on top. For a moment it flashed through my mind that I ought to get out of here, that this was nothing at all to do with me, but for one thing I couldn't remember exactly how to get home from there, and for another there wouldn't have been time, because from the terrified look on Little Tibi's face it was clear that his father had at that very moment come into the room and seen at once that there was something wrong.

We didn't have much explaining to do. He took one look at the floor and immediately realised what had happened. He said nothing, but stepped over the turned-over lino, and leaning against the door-post, opened another bottle of beer.

"Perhaps they'll be okay with the green. Or not. Stuff 'em."

On the way home in the van we were silent and he only once said anything, or rather, to be more precise, he let slip something from his deepest thoughts as he screeeched to a stop on red at the last minute:

"How many of them were there?"

"How many of who?" asked Little Tibi from the back as he ripped pieces of sticking tape off his hands.

"How many inspectors?"

"Two."

"I thought so. They always go around in twos."

After that we said nothing more. Outside it had gone completely dark, the thousands of lights on the receding estate had come on, and the cars' headlights blazed white.

That night I had a dream but then woke with an unexpectedly intense awareness that we were leaving the following morning, though not from their place: they'd be picking me up by car. If they came at all, that is, after we'd screwed up the flooring. And after I'd left the new tickets I'd taken to show them on the lacquered table in the lounge. They'd be thrown away, or just disappear. I managed to go back to sleep but at a deeper, darker level than before my roving hand once again found its way to the switch of consciousness and suddenly, as I lay there, I came out with a sentence from the far side: "I should at least have kept the Romanian one with me."

At about this point, in the coolest and darkest hours of the night, when the concrete highways gleam white in the moonlight, and the blind, black blocks of the sleeping estate rise into a starless sky, when the parking lots' puddles glimmer with a dull sheen, and there's no humming of wheels, not a sound to be heard anywhere, when the silence purrs in sleeping brains like a switched-off TV, when every window looking out onto the courtyard is dark, that was when Big Tibi stepped onto the topmost rung of the ladder.

He had to shake his son for a long time before he opened his eyes, though even then he was still not really awake. He sat up, staring blankly into the dark, from which he saw emerging, slowly, very gradually, the outline of his father's face, and had great difficulty understanding a sentence that seemed to come from a long way off:

"Don't think those folk won't find you. 'Cause they will, for sure."

COLD FLOOR

(BASELINE)

It's a thirteen-hour flight. I unfold the red blanket and pick up the earpieces laid out on the seat. Meanwhile the Japanese man next to me is also settling down: with a practised movement he kicks off his shoes and puts on his linen sleep mask. He fidgets about for a bit, then nods off. I start reading David Scott's travel guide: "Japan is a rather expensive country, but the baseline of services everywhere is so high that even if we stay in the most modest hotels, dine in restaurants favoured by the locals, and travel only on public transport, we will find it impeccable." Oh, come now. I close the book and browse through the films on offer. The alien body asleep beside me makes me feel rather uncomfortable: it's as if we were in the marital bed and my ad hoc husband's little snores indicated he was unhappy I was watching TV in the middle of the night. Outside it is growing steadily darker and we leave behind the soft cottonwool clouds, which from inside the plane look like an endless blanket of thick snow.

I keep clicking through the films on offer and eventually settle on *The Island*. We see Scarlett Johansson running around a futuristic interior in white dungarees, then a swimming pool with perfect young bodies relaxing around it. It occurs to me that on this flight perhaps *Lost in Translation* would be more appropriate. I remember Bill Murray with the clamps he forgot to remove from the back of his jacket and burst out laughing, whereupon my neighbour stirs, grimaces, and then the lines on his face smooth out again.

I envy him. I try to sleep, turning my head towards the window and resting my temple against the top of the seat. I step out into the soft blanket of grey snow, I move further and further away from the plane, as if re-enacting the moon landing. Lights glint in the distance, perhaps the lit-up windows of a town in space to which I am drawn by the little flickering blue lights of my dreamtime walk. I repeatedly bounce along the candyfloss terrain. I'm flying, with wings outspread I let my weightless body be swept along in the airstream. The pilot's voice startles me awake: we have reached our cruising height, the temperature outside is minus 74 degrees Centigrade. My legs are cold, it's no use trying to cover them with the blanket. I stick the earpieces back into my ears and resume watching the film. We walk into an enormous room in which bodies are lying in endless rows, as if sleeping in a position in which they were lying to attention, with their eyes open and their expressionless faces staring at the screens horizontally above them. Clones, untouched bodies lacking any history, mass produced vessels in the form of human beings that absorb the multiplicity of images streaming into the pupils of their eyes. I took a sleeping pill but it was no use and I couldn't return to the dream I had managed eventually to find. I move the seat back a little and pretend to be a clone myself, a body without a past or a future, flown by some vehicle cruising through the black void towards the unknown. I am without thoughts, feeling or pain, I forget about the pullover folded under the nape of my neck and the man huffing and snorting beside me and, taking deep breaths, I eventually manage to find my way back onto that plumped up inside track.

I find it difficult to come to, the blanket has slid off, my legs have gone completely numb. I have to gather my stuff. There is a long queue in the corridors of Narita airport. I'm desperately hunting for my passport: there are now only two people ahead of me. I'd put it in the travel guide, along with the tickets and the hard currency. I have to unpack everything on the ground, a hairbrush falls out, and now I see I've also brought the earpieces from the plane. Never mind. There's a low-browed woman behind the glass partition. She glances at the passport, then looks me in the face, right between the eyes, a small area in my brain heats up where her look stabs me. Our glances meet. It is a fraction of a second, an unconscionably brief moment, but long enough for the seismograph in the deepest recesses of my consciousness to be activated, for a feeling to well up from somewhere in the pit of my stomach and signal: it's going to happen. I don't know exactly *what*, and it doesn't even matter, but it's the same thing that has occurred hundreds of thousands, even millions of times: I know the words with which it will end, as if you were trying to utter words you know so well that you're bored with them, making the attempt, again, for the thousandth time, to utter them all the way to the end, amidst all the set-changes, the costumes your destiny has worn at various times, sometimes well-fitting, sometimes not.

"Please take a step forward."

"Kindly come with me."

"You can put that down."

"Go in there."

I have been sitting in a space surrounded by reinforced glass walls, entirely see-through, for I don't know how long. In front of the door a female droid with a machine gun stands guard. It doesn't reply to my questions, it doesn't open the door; my knocks and bangings don't even make it turn around. I'm dying for a pee, I'm hungry, I have a headache, I don't know the address of my hotel, I want to get the woman standing guard to ring the embassy, to get my hand luggage back, to get them to speak to the Japanese gentleman who is supposed to meet me and is perhaps still waiting for me, I want them to apologise, I want the whole improbable, nightmarish misunderstanding be sorted out. I have no idea how much time has passed: my phone is in my hand luggage.

"Please. Please! Please!!!" I plead in English.

I bang on the glass in vain, the armed silhouette does not stir. Outside someone passes by, I try to attract their attention; they don't even cast a glance in my direction. It occurs to me suddenly that I should just squat down and pee. Or perhaps do a shit. Or perhaps both – that's it, both a pee and a shit. But I haven't got the nerve. I stand up, and then lie down along the plexiglass bench, to demonstrate that this incarcerated body, tired and tense from holding in her pee, is not inclined to sit and wait in a disciplined manner. The bench is uncomfortable and makes my side ache. The female droid, as if she had eyes in the back of her head, immediately turns around and comes in.

Wake up, please. Sit on the bench, she says in English.

I notice that two other people are being shepherded towards the glass-walled room. The moment the door closes behind them they introduce themselves. They are equally at a loss as to why they have been brought in, but appear neither particularly surprised nor aggrieved. They tell me it's half past ten, which means I've been sitting here for two hours. The Portuguese woman starts nibbling at something from the paper bag in her pocket, between crunchy bites briefly directing crunchy English sentences in our direction. The Cameroonian fellow has not had his bag taken away: he takes out a book and starts reading. He is suddenly raised up from among us, enveloped in a transparent cocoon of freedom, like a glass cube inside a glass cube. He looks up only occasionally and glances at his watch, only to bury himself in his book again. The Portuguese woman has finished her roll and is now adjusting her lipstick. I come out with very silly sentences, along the lines of: I'm a literature scholar, I've come for a conference. My voice sounds to me as if it were coming from outside my body, I feel ashamed, but press on: *I am tourist, I write poems. I am invited... to a... congress... to a literature congress.* The Portuguese woman smiles indulgently. My bladder is about to burst.

After three and a quarter hours, the droid enters and asks me to follow her. She takes me to a small table where my briefcase stands, zipped up. It hasn't been opened, they ask no questions, offer no explanations, just hand me back my passport.

"Enjoy your time in Japan!"

I scour the room for a toilet. Two people are unexpectedly helpful and point to the far corner of the vast terminal. This makes me think that perhaps I've already wet myself and maybe can't even feel that there's a dark pee-stain on the back of my skirt.

My suitcase has to be located in the baggage store on the basis of the label. *Yes, yes.* That's the one. I set off for the exit. I feel that my steps are frighteningly light, perhaps I'm not even here. It may be just a dream after all. In fact, it's certain: I'm no longer hungry, my pain has gone, time is suspended, not a single clock on the gleaming marble walls. I wander round in a circle, a lost presence. At customs the guard makes me go to one side. He pulls my suitcase over and signals to the armed guard standing a little way off. They gesture to me to follow them.

We are headed straight for the place from where ten minutes earlier they had let me go.

The two in uniform are still standing there by the table. They nod and lift up my suitcase, bending over it like doctors taking a first, preliminary glance at a swollen belly. Suddenly I have what I think is a splendid idea. I turn politely to one of those in uniform, the one that had earlier given me back my passport:

"Excuse me, sir, does anyone here speak French?"

The other one looks out for a moment from behind the raised suitcase lid, as its multicoloured, jumbled up innards flash into view, looks at me, and replies, in flawless French:

"Non, Madame, je suis désolé. Ici personne ne parle pas français."

He achieves his goal. Suddenly, before I realise it, my tears start to flow of their own accord. I have no tissues and can't wipe them away. I watch as they take out the underwiring from my bras, one bra at a time. As they break up the effervescent vitamin C tablets on the table. As they slice open the suitcase's faux-silk lining. As they pat down, sniff up, smooth down, pull out, rummage about, scratch around, turn things inside out. It will all be over soon. My eye make-up is dripping, my nose is running. And that was all there was to it. But no, there is, after all, a small role for me to play, for a few seconds. In an outside pocket one of them finds a bag with red plastic hair curlers in it. He takes it out and looks at me questioningly. I've not the faintest why I brought these, what I could have had in mind when I packed them, but it now feels good to get my own back for the tears I shed in front of them. I pick up one of the curlers and, almost cheerfully, show them how you slip it onto your cock, like that, carefully, that's what it's for. It looks as if the droids don't come with a built-in humour detector: the face of the one in the uniform remains impassive and he proceeds to take out every little cylinder from the bag and to inspect them all, one by one.

When he has finished doing this, the previous leave-taking is repeated:

"Enjoy your time in Japan!"

I shouldn't have come here. I have no business in this country. I head back to customs, dragging behind me the eviscerated, tortured and gutted suitcase, with the clothes jampacked in it and the books splayed open, their spines throbbing. I step out into the sunshine: it's past midday, traffic is thundering along the streets and it feels as if I've taken a step from the sepulchral silence of the grave into the pulsating land of the living. Opposite the exit stands the man sent to meet me, and on an impossibly large, poster-sized card there is my name, loud and clear.

Exspectatus sum, ergo sum. He bows deeply and flashes me a radiant smile. He has spent four and a half hours on the pavement and will probably be unable to straighten out his right arm today. He asks if there was some problem. I shake my head: nothing serious, but my head moves so easily on my neck that I stop shaking it and just give a dumb smile. I've just noticed I must be missing a vertebra.

"I'd like to change some money," I say quietly.

"But of course."

We walk over to a little window in a wall some way off, where you have to strike a bell on the counter. A low-browed woman comes out and asks me for my papers. I stick my passport through the window and then start rummaging in my hand luggage. Ah, there's David Scott's travel guide ("Japan is a rather expensive country, but the baseline of services everywhere is so high that even if we stay in the most modest hotels, dine in restaurants favoured by the locals, and travel only on public transport, we will find it impeccable."). My return ticket is inside the guide and, of course, that's where I find the open packet of tissues, too – why couldn't I get my hands on that before. Never mind. I take out the envelope marked "hard currency". There's three hundred euro in it, saved up from my earlier trips.

Three years ago, when we were still in love, we went to Italy. When I see the envelope I recall the entire Italian trip, I recall my love, with whom we invented the most loving game I have ever played in my life: the twelve little slips spread out on the hotel table, to be turned over one at a time, with a wish for each evening.

All this had happened three years ago, and how quickly they had passed: some of the slips remained as they were, never turned over. Confused images crowd my mind, about the rows we had and the shouting match on the dark and murky shores of the Arno, on our last night, as it turned into a shivery dawn filled with bitter recriminations.

I fill in the form, three hundred euros, yes, in hundred-euro notes. I tear open the envelope. Instead of money, there tumble from the envelope those slips of paper, home-made banknotes of our love, unused tokens withdrawn from circulation. The first, that I didn't in the end pass over to the low-browed woman, has written on it: *Lick my navel.*

We head downtown. I look at the tiny houses lining the road, nodding off for a few minutes now and then. Every airport has a road just like this leading to it, a road several lanes wide linking the no man's land of the outskirts with the beating heart of the centre of town, lined with shabby, tightly packed single-storey buildings, with clothes drying outside, mysterious little windows, the stage sets of alien lives. My tired gaze registers the curious roofs, the tiny windows with their bamboo shutters.

We soon reach the hotel. The enormous tower block is surrounded by several similar slabs, and I immediately feel lost. While the man accompanying me and the receptionist are busy checking me in, I buy a sandwich at the snack bar, as I simply don't have the strength to go and sit down in the restaurant.

My room is on the nineteenth floor. The sound-insulated and permanently locked window looks out onto an identical building. I stare at the buttons sunk into the wall and uncertainly press one of them. The electronic shutter comes down, the room goes dark. My name appears on the TV screen: Welcome! I feel welcomed, as it's no longer completely dark. I press another button: music. I come to my senses and quickly insert the keycard where it's supposed to go, so I can now turn on the lighting. There's light again and I confidently press the button I pressed before, but instead of the shutter rolling up, some kind of mood lighting built into the walls comes on. Well, let's have another go and try the row of buttons below. The shutter glides up with a hum. So far, so good: it's all going swimmingly, I can make it light and make it go dark, only the order it happens in is random. Now, let's just see about the temperature. There are two buttons. I press one twice, then kick off my shoes and stretch out on the bed.

I wake to the realisation that I am very cold. The room has gone freezing cold, while outside it's evening, with little pinpricks of light filling the void. My hands have gone impossibly stiff, I must have set the air conditioning virtually to freezing. I quickly take a shower, with the water mysteriously alternating between hot and cold, then go down to reception, but only after a little run-around between the four lifts, because the one I position myself to take invariably happens to be going up.

Behind the desk a man in glasses keeps bowing courteously. He is determined to take my magnetic keycard, but I resist. He smiles unrelentingly.

"I'm sorry I don't know how does the air conditioner work. I did ... something wrong ...and ... it is too cold in the room." I rub my arm, to make even clearer what the problem is. The man with glasses at once asks someone to take over behind the desk and accompanies me to my room. As we enter he can't help giving a rather brazen

grin: obviously I'm not the first tourist to refrigerate themselves. He presses one of the buttons in the wall twice, then backs out of the room bowing repeatedly and I, instead of attending to my suitcase, begin arranging the newly-found slips of paper.

It's as if this was why I came here. In some obscure way I'd felt for weeks, indeed months, that I had unfinished business with this feeling of mine, that it would surface in the most unexpected, most impossible situations, that it isn't possible to simply end a relationship just like that, that I would have to work hard at turning into the past a time that was still present and still haunting me, on which I had still not closed the door behind me.

Surveying the twelve requests as a batch, I have to say that while my lover's sentences – with one exception – formulate rather specific desires, my messages by contrast bespeak some kind of absence or lack that it was impossible to specify or fulfil: as if the task I had assigned him was nothing less than to fill all the cracks that had formed upon the carapace of my existence up until then. Looking back, sitting on a double bed at the other end of the world, I now suddenly understand why he was always talking about mutability, why he felt that his personality had in fact disappeared in the crazy vortex of love that had sucked in the essence of his being. It now dawns on me that passion of such intensity is ultimately depersonalising, that someone of whom you demand everything is in the end unable to give you anything, because they can no longer be sure that it is their true self that is reflected in the whirling surface of another soul.

Stay with me for ever.

What nonsense. That was, of course, one of mine. I lie back, as if suddenly unable to take any more, then sit up and arrange the twelve slips into two piles. On the very top comes *May it never be so good with anyone else*. That's at least as crazy as mine: a curse rather than a wish, with more desperation in it than desire. On the bed lie two sets of six slips of paper, face down. It can't be mere chance that these slips have ended up coming here with me. One by one I turn them the right way up. I have to find somewhere to put these words that we once wrote, to find them all a final resting place.

The next morning I am standing at the gateway of a nearby Shinto shrine, a map of the city in my hand, the slips of paper in my pocket. I want to find a place, first of all, for my lover's most ardent slip of paper: that's the task I have set myself for this morning. I look around, somewhat at a loss as to what to do. The request is explicit and passionate, but at the same time, written out like this, it's quite embarrassingly stupid. I intend to put it in the most secret place possible. A warm nook, protected for ever. I walk into the shrine's park, its entrance guarded by two lions. The mouth of the one on the right is wide open, symbolising life; the mouth of the other is closed, as that is the lion of death. I wander around in the jinja's park, watching the locals. They arrive, wash their hands, and enter the shrine. Their every movement reflects some kind of diligent effort: perhaps they have indeed come for only a few minutes. I am just taking a picture of the golden leaves of a ginkgo when a flock of white doves takes to the air from the canopy. Doves! I spend some time wondering how I might entrust this most ardent of my slips to a white dove, so that a surprised monk might receive the no longer valid message written in a foreign tongue. Nonsense; I have to find some simpler way. All of a sudden I have the solution: I'll place the paper slip in the mouth of the lion that represents life, so that the next day it will breathe fire and stun the pedestrians all around with its blazing red eyes. And so I set off to return but suddenly stop in my tracks. I see opposite, on a string stretched between two posts, a flurry of white pieces of paper fluttering in the wind. As if the close relatives of my own slips were trembling on the string: pristine strips of snow white. These are called nusha and signify purity. The purity of the absence of desire. I walk over and without further ado tie one of slips to the string: *Caress my breasts.*

I sense that what I'm doing is in a certain sense inappropriate, but at the same time I'm aware of the cultic character of what I have done, so for that reason I don't permit the smidgin of doubt simmering in my consciousness to get a word in edgeways.

On the way out I glance back and say farewell to that desire of three years ago. The scrap with the tiny letters on it is lost among its virgin companions, and perhaps I wouldn't even be able to find it if I had a sudden urge to retrieve it.

I arrive back at the entrance: from close up, the stone lion appears a tougher nut to crack. Its fine, big, wide-open mouth is at least a couple of metres up, so in order to put my slip in it I'd have to climb up the creature somehow. Geekily I start taking photographs while I examine it more closely to see if there are any suitable projections I could use. The streets are unusually busy, as it's the lunch hour and people from the offices nearby are pouring out onto the streets.

I spend so much time taking pictures of the lion that it's becoming noticeable, or at least I feel it is. Were someone to come up to me I'd say I just wanted to see if it had a tongue. After all, there are silly tourists everywhere and what I happen to be interested in is specifically lions' tongues: that in itself is hardly a crime. I imagine how back home a Japanese tourist might clamber up to one of the stone lions on our Chain Bridge, but then I realise that it's not quite the same thing: it's more as if he wanted to look – let's say – inside the head of a statue of the Virgin.

On the spur of the moment I put my camera in my pocket and start to climb. No one pays me the slightest bit of attention and I'm face to face with the dragon-like visage when I realise that as I am clinging on with both hands, I can't take the envelope out of my pocket and, even if I could, I'd have to use my mouth to lift out that most ardent of the slips, which – hmm – while as far as its content was concerned wouldn't be contrary to the spirit of where I wished to place it, in practice the task seemed impossible to carry out. What a fool I am. I climb down, get the slip ready, and clamber back. Down below a little girl stops in her tracks and holding her mother's hand stares up at me. She's bound to be told it's not something that's allowed, but I can't turn back: I'm right in front of my goal, just a little stretch and my finger can touch the inward-curled tongue. It's in, I've done it. I jump down and give the little girl a reassuring smile, though I've hurt my knee – I shouldn't have jumped down from so high up. Her mother drags the little girl away and suddenly I feel very tired. I leave the lion with the spicy, burning alienness of the sentence: let him taste it in his mouth. It was a fine piece of work, quick work, a work of mourning.

The following day I make a pilgrimage to the Asakusa Kannon temple. Flanking the main entrance are two statues in booths, in front of them a wire fence. I choose the statue of Lightning, inserting by its feet one of the slips: *Kiss my spine all the way down.* Later I regret my decision, Lightning would have deserved a different sentence, but then I recall what it felt like when he actually kissed my spine all the way down and realise that the piece of paper at the feet of thunder and lightning is, after all, in the right place.

I must buy presents for the kid, it would be best to do that today. Tired, I take the underground aimlessly, and then at Takebashi station I crumple up into a ball one of the slips I'd taken out at the shrine and flick it in front of a train. I act quickly, like a suicide, and *May it never be so good with anyone else* has already disappeared under the wheels of a train just rolling in. I get a dirty look from a shrivelled old lady, who takes me for a litter lout of a tourist.

I go a couple of stops and end up at the toy department of a gigantic store. I pass a wall of remote-controlled, battery-operated robots: they move, flash, shoot. My shoes have blistered my feet and I need to buy a plaster. I can't see any sensible presents, I wander around growing more and more faint among the fearful creatures. On a shelf opposite there stands a row of piggy banks.

Suddenly I have an idea. I run a scenario in my head: a Japanese boy, on reaching his thirteenth birthday, goes into his room and smashes up his piggy bank. I don't know where I got the thirteen years from, but for some reason I cling to this fantasy and it doesn't even occur to me that the piggy bank could be a little girl's. I never had a piggy bank myself, somehow it's boys that generally save, for a bike or a skateboard, that sort of thing. My slip of paper would be found by a thirteen-year-old boy: I believe this with utter, and absurd, certainty.

I go over to the piggy banks and imagine how one solemn day in the distant future among the coins to be counted there crops up a slip of paper written in an alien tongue:

Tell me about your most secret desires.

My choice falls on a spotted ceramic cow. I look round, as if doing something forbidden, and casually drop the slip of paper into it, then steal away from the toy department. Later it occurs to me that security may be nonplussed by footage from the CCTV and will never know what on earth that European woman was up to.

I must go back to the hotel to change my shoes and think through the next stage of my schedule: I have seven slips of paper left and tomorrow I'll be halfway through my stay here, a dividing line, a trough. The saddest sentence keeps going around my head. This one will be next day's task, the one that will have to be buried somewhere, so that I can at last bury it in myself, too.

Back in the hotel I carefully portion out the things I have to do and plan the future scenarios, leaving room for spontaneous possibilities as well. I find extraordinarily moving the sentence *Caress me with your hair.* It resembles somewhat my own desires, a gentle, loving whisper from another evening. I decide to let it fly away in the wind tomorrow, provided there is indeed some wind, for until now there has been only a certain amount of languid sunshine warming the motionless air.

I get up from the breakfast table the following day at eight-thirty, wait until the gesticulating Americans have ordered their taxis, and gently inquire at reception:

"Sorry, does the wind blow here? I mean... is there any... wind?"

The same man with glasses is on duty as on the previous day. At first he is surprised by the question but then looks up and recognises me with a smile: ah, the woman who had temperature issues. Obviously he thinks I have an immune deficiency, or am asthmatic, or the like. So many of them around these days. He smiles as he carefully articulates his reply:

"We have a nice day. So the weather is pleasant today. I can assure you that the wind is not blowing today."

So the slip that will have to be dealt with today is the sad one. The saddest one of all. That one, and the one in the bath, though that will be easy to deal with.

I head for the river bank, on foot as far as the bridge leading to the Imperial Palace. I would like to get closer to the river, but everywhere a handrail keeps you away from the steep embankment. It's a somewhat banal solution, but the slip *Let's have a bath together* I simply want to throw into the water. The paper is too light, it should be tied to something. I don't have string or a hairgrip with me. In the end I look among the bushes and find a stick: that's it! It has a split end where I insert the slip, then I take a swing back and throw it into the apparently motionless river. It doesn't drift away but swirls around on the water's surface with interminable slowness, then comes to a stop.

How hard it is to cut oneself free of desire.

I turn round and walk back by the bushes lining the main road. The crows are strange hereabouts: the feathers on their crowns are short, which makes them all look as if they have had a brush cut. They waddle along inquisitively beside me. I'm getting more and more nervous: my heart is pounding because of the task ahead. Finally I stop dithering, crouch down by a cone shape that has formed around a tree and start digging around it in the soil. I'm working with a twig, but the soil is compacted and it's hard to make the tiny ditch even a little deeper. Runners in trainers and wearing earpieces jog past me, as apparently this spot lies on their regular route. Suddenly I have the feeling that I'm being watched: a man walking his dog is staring at me, even bending over slightly, watching me as I dig with his head tilted to one side. I get the feeling that he wants to be of assistance: he must think I have lost something. I look up amiably to indicate that everything is fine and I'd prefer it if folk just went past, they are disturbing me in my mourning. When finally they resume their walk and I look at them, I notice that the man is wearing the same kind of knitted blue pullover as his dog. A flash of insight: the doggie must have wanted to answer a call of nature, this is his favourite place, and here I am, crouched down over it. I walk round the tree to check there is no dog poo anywhere, then pile some pebbles on top of the slip of paper I have buried.

That's it, I'm done. I move on. Barely visible even from a few yards away is the little hump under which rests the saddest slip of all: *I want to have your children.*

Very late in the evening I take a seat in a packed restaurant in the shopping mall. On the trays of the noisy young folk having dinner before me I note somewhat languidly the aesthetically designed cups and trays. I am a lone, late diner. I can see the kitchen staff in the corridor leaving one by one. Yet the servers aren't hurrying me and continue to bring out the random dishes I have ordered in good humour and at a steady pace. When I've finished, I put one of the slips on the tray, like some kind of very special tip. This was my lover's second most ardent sentence, though it's possible that others might have put them in a different order and that they'd have put tonight's slip after the one that went into the lion. It crosses my mind that there are Hungarians everywhere, my fellow countrymen are liable to turn up in the most surprising and unexpected corners of the world, and I imagine the horrified employee as he returns and slaps the tray down in front of me with the message on it. But no, that's absurd: the server quite certainly doesn't understand the words on the slip. I am still wondering about this when my tray is unexpectedly whisked away. All my worries were unwarranted: the young lad doesn't deign to give the slip – or even me – a glance. A few seconds later he is back and I pay. I have two days' money left and four sentences.

Getting to Mount Fuji is not as straightforward as I imagined. In the morning a young woman at the desk explains how many times I have to change on the underground to get to the railway station. In four hours you can get quite close to the mountain by train. But I don't want to get close, I want to actually be there. Perhaps that's the problem, this wanting everything; it ought to be enough to get near things, but for me, I want the volcano, the crater itself.

This is how I ruin everything for myself. As the woman marks every station on a photocopy, I become quite despondent. It's only in the soil of the volcano that *Stay with me for ever* can rest, but if I can't actually reach the mountain, what's the point of setting off at all? I thank her profusely for the photocopy, bow, and turn as if to leave the hallway without further ado for Mount Fuji. I wouldn't want to cause her any disappointment. Then, reaching the bustle of the street, I turn round and head instead for a playground nearby.

A little boy is being taught how to walk by his mother: the child happily toddles his way towards her and as he does so the stocky woman repeats a short word every time. I spend a long time looking at them and, scouring the benches, realise the game must wait. As a matter of fact I'm looking for the right place to put *Dance for me*, but I'm out of ideas. In the afternoon, in the garden of a small Buddhist shrine I discover an odd-looking statue of a panda. The wooden statue is hollow at the back, carved out like a washtub. *Lick my navel* ends up in the panda's mouth, rolled up rather like a cigarette. It's not the smartest solution, I can see that myself, but I think it will do. That desire, when I think about it, was rather startling: I wonder what could have got into me that evening in Italy, when all my life my I've had a ticklish stomach? I don't know pandas' attitudes to this kind of thing, but for this sentence I would never have found an ideal spot anyway. *Dance for me* ultimately ends up in the hollow trunk of a tree: a message to the motionless foliage, sender unknown.

I spend the following day in the Tokyo National Museum, and in the evening I lie on my bed, exhausted. I flick through the channels on the TV. I'm tired, the rapidly changing scenes on the TV are continually overwritten by scenes from my past life, though the statues I have seen during the day keep haunting me, until I finally fall asleep to the voice of a newscaster gabbling away in English. The envelope, which still has two slips left in it, I put on the upholstered shelf above the bed, between a box of tissues and the travel guide. "Japan is a rather expensive country, but the level of service everywhere is so high that even if we stay in the most modest hotels, dine in restaurants favoured by the locals, and travel only on public transport, we will find it impeccable."

I'm still fully dressed as I'm overcome by sleep, and manage to shed my jeans only as day breaks. In the morning I'm surprised to see that the envelope is no longer where I left it. I have just fifteen minutes before they stop serving breakfast, so I hurriedly get dressed and rush down to the dining room. I'm sure I'll find it when I get back. I must have put something else on top of it. Back in my room I change the battery in my camera and then pat my way along the bed. A cleaner interrupts me, her arms piled high with fresh towels. She is very determined, but I indicate to her that I want to sleep and she departs with a nod.

The envelope is nowhere to be found. It has simply disappeared. Then I notice there's a gap between the wall and the little shelf: it's slipped into that. I attempt to pull the bed away but the shelf and the upholstered headboard are of a piece and I'd have to tear the whole unit away from the wall. It's probably where they've put the wiring for the built-in lights: that's what's hidden behind the velour-covered wood. So that's where the envelope will stay, only to be found one day when the room is refurbished, or if there's an electrical fault. *Stay with me for ever, Caress me with your hair.* As a matter of fact, here behind the bed is not such a bad place for them. A couple of Japanese electricians will shrug their shoulders when they see my envelope – they may even hand it in at reception, or an annoyed chambermaid will try to pull out of the nozzle of a wheezing vacuum cleaner the pieces of paper it has sucked in.

You can't tell when any of this might happen. Whether it'll be far in the future, perhaps in many years' time, that they will pick up the crumpled envelope with the – to them – meaningless sentences in it, or maybe as soon as next week. I have to bide my time. That's when my mourning will be over. I will sense when the final sentence will be passing out of me, along with the anger I felt at the airport. The pain will pass, the feeling of having been hurt, and only the white places of desire will shine forth, like the virgin white streamers of the nusha.

On my last day it's pouring with rain. The wind has started up as well, but it's too late, I'm ready, I've already completed the fortuitous mission. I keep thinking, as I fight my way to the underground station with an umbrella tuned inside out by the wind, that I could have kept something back for the rain.

The cone around the tree comes to mind, the message under the little heap of pebbles slowly turning to mush, and I am reassured. All's well. The storm has come at a good time, and so has the wind.

In the evening, soaked through, I reach my room utterly exhausted. I undress and, teeth chattering, bury myself in the blanket, but find it impossible to get warm. I keep pressing the button as I'd like it to heat up a bit before I fall asleep.

On the morning of my departure I wake up barely able to breathe. The heat in the room is stifling, quite unbearable, and the daylight outside is improbably bright. I don't know when or how I could have clambered down from the bed: I am lying on my back on the cold floor, my kimono undone.

I am a clone: a perfect replica of my unhistoried self, of wounds and pains, a timeless hollow body. Into my wide-open eyes someone from above, from the twentieth floor, is projecting onto the ceiling the scenes of my life hitherto, my memories-to-be.

"THE WITCH HAS THREE, THREE KIDS HAS SHE"

(THE LINE'S BUSY)

Let's start with the stove. It's covered with big, caramel-coloured tiles that are shiny like the brittle glaze on the top of a dobos torte. From close to, you can even make out the hairline cracks on their surface. The stove of my childhood was like this, in our very first home. I remember I was four and quite unable to understand what it meant to *move house*. I wasn't clear about the meaning of the words. My father thrust a big nylon carrier into my hand and told me to put in it all the toys I wanted to take with me. Because we were moving house. I pottered around clueless amid the chaos: the contents of the row of mass-produced Varia wardrobes that had been moved away from their usual place lay scattered on the floor, my mother ran agitatedly to and fro with the rubbish to the outside corridor, while I sat on the floor leisurely stuffing building blocks into the carrier. By the following morning everything was ready.

My father pointed to the blanket lying on the floor and the naked doll: What about these? You don't want them? No, I shook my head, and dragged the carrier, which I held by its opening, around the empty room. When I looked up again, I could see only that my father was stuffing the doll, legs first, into the stove, after the rags. You could see how these caught fire amid the orange glow of the embers, the doll taking only seconds to shrivel up into something unrecognisable, though the rags flopped about as their edges disintegrated into separate strands and glowed until my father slammed the stove's iron door on them.

The screaming could be heard in the outside corridor, someone had moved house out of me, never to return.

The new place was not that bad, actually: I met little Imi from next door, and we fell in love and decided there and then we would be man and wife when we grew up. And have three children. It didn't appear to be out of the question: life seemed to have prospects, despite the flames blazing in the stove, though tripping across the mist-shrouded fields of maize and that October night did not feature in it. To sum up, the way it was envisaged when wearing a white net curtain veil at the kindergarten fancy dress party was not precisely how things turned out, though if you look at the figures overall, the balance sheet is about even. I did have a son, there was true love after all, with Imruska: though it was slow in coming, come it did, and blazed with a great flame in what was already a blazing hot summer that never seemed to want to end. Even in October it was hot, the sunshine so improbably strong that my tee-shirt got soaked through on the trolleybus I took to the hospital, and behind my sunglasses my face was steamy with sweat.

There was a long wait at gynaecology: no matter that I had an appointment, even the doctor hadn't yet arrived, and there were already four women waiting out in the corridor. None of them looked pregnant – I suppose I didn't either, though by then I'd repeated the test several times and was sure that the hitherto unseen, round and beaming face would soon be visible to the whole world.

At first I didn't take in what the doctor was saying: he kept pointing to the monitor and saying with a smile that I should just look; then he amplified the double heartbeat. That one was, in fact, two. Or rather, if you include the one we already had, three. It was improbable and a little frightening, too. I couldn't imagine myself as a mother of three: that really was something else, another body, another life. I flung on my clothes behind the screen, stuffing my tights into my bag, as it was so hot anyway.

As I made may way along Dózsa György Street, crossing the side streets one after the other, perhaps as many as three trolleybuses rumbled past. I continued as I basked in the golden glow towards Ajtósi Dürer Row, planning the sentence, the sentence I would say to him on the phone, which would be followed by a long silence and ecstatic surprise, the sentence that I had once already imagined and composed, but which I now had to recast in my head, adjusting it to the bodies mysteriously growing in me, which I imagined right from the outset were twin boys.

The line was busy. I rang later: still busy. He'd gone out to clear his head a bit, write his lecture, and turn off the hosepipe in the garden, because it was quite possible we wouldn't be able to go down to the cottage again before winter set in. The cottage nestled at the very end of a dead-end village, on the edge of the fields, in a remote corner of Nógrád county, with nothing beyond it but the forest and the endless sky. I rang his mobile; it was turned off. I imagined him in a tee-shirt raking in the leaves in the garden. I always told him there was no point, but for some reason he was keen to sweep up the leaves from the apple and the walnut trees. He liked to chop wood for kindling, invariably chopping up much more than was needed for the rare winter weekends we spent there. I pictured him chopping the wood and piling the logs neatly in the shed, I pictured him having a cup of coffee outside the house,

I pictured him and I loved him. Even in the evening the line was busy, and the next morning, too. From midday I rang every half-hour. My love was busy.

Busy, busy, busy. In the afternoon I sat in the gloaming and mentally began to pack, but my body did not stir. The afternoon sun on the veranda felt good, and I knew there was not much longer to wait, as the last bus left around six, so at about quarter to six I could calm down, put on a cardigan, and stare at the room. To think about where you might put two small beds.

I couldn't. At seven I called the bus station. There's a bus at eight-thirty, said the voice at the other end. It only stops twice and is in Terenye by eleven. But you'd have to walk the rest of the way. No problem, I said, I've often done that, though it was true that had been in the summer and in daylight, but surely in the cool of the evening an hour's walk wouldn't be that tiring.

I also rang my son, who was at his grandmother's, as if I were planning a longish trip. I didn't say I was taking the evening bus, as they were bound to talk me out of it, I thought. I didn't say anything about anything else either; there was plenty of time, I reflected, as the longer conversation I planned to have with my son about his siblings-to-be was scheduled for later. I called my best friend, too, saying only that I had to go on a trip.

"Don't go down to the cottage," she said with unusual emphasis, which only made me even keener to go.

They always kept a spare key to the house in the restaurant in Terenye. The bus was almost empty; I dozed off and the driver had to turn round and shout twice that we'd arrived. By this time it was pitch dark outside and suddenly I had a frightening thought as I clambered down from the bus: what if there's no one in? I hurried along the highway and could see from far off that that there were still folk at the inn. There was very little traffic, just the odd car heading towards Tarján, its headlights blinding me. It was getting cooler. The door of the inn was already locked, but the lights were on inside. I knocked long and loud on the door. The waiter, who knew who I was, finally opened upand was astonished as he took some time to register that it was me.

As we stood facing each other, I gazed in stupefaction at the pale and bemused fellow and tried to interpret his expression. The whole story was written on his face, all one had to do was was make out what it said; it would have been best to just let him get over his confusion and say something, or invite me in for a drink. I sensed what he wanted to say, so rather than let him say anything, I asked him, quietly but firmly, for the key. His slightly alarmed question seemed to reach me from a long way away, and hung in the air:

"Would you ... like me to drive you over?"

I made may way along the highway with long, even steps and taking deep breaths, like someone preparing for a long-distance walking race. I just carried on, inhaling and exhaling, and when at last the village came into view, broke into a run. I ran over the embankment and over the ditch, past the houses with their darkened windows, leaving the lit-up church behind me, stumbling across the misty, pitch-dark maize fields, I ran and ran, sweat pouring off me in rivulets. Then I caught sight of the house from quite far away, and came to a sudden stop.

Once my heartbeat had steadied, I lit a cigarette and drew the smoke deep into my lungs as I stared, through the cold air, at the picket fence and the door of our house. I completely forgot about the news I was bringing and because of which I ought not, of course, to have been smoking. I took out the mobile once more, for the last time, to ring our number. My beloved. Busy. I dialled his number: still switched off. I stood and felt cold. On the way the handle of my canvas bag had come off. Slowly I made for the house. The light in the back room was on. I knocked on the entrance door, and pressing my face to the glass tried to peer inside. He took a long time coming to the door, trying to figure out who might be standing outside in the dark. He switched on a light, his familiar naked body covered only by a towel around his waist. We stood there, neither of us saying a word. In the sudden silence my panting was quite audible.

"You?" he said.

I was speechless. I could see someone making their way out from the inside room and coming to the door. A blonde woman stood there in a dressing gown, her big breasts flopping out. She stopped behind him; they seemed to be almost the same height, and in fact the camera that continued to roll in my head independently of my conscious mind even registered that the woman had varnished toenails. The whole thing was like some improbable film, in which we happened to be playing the main roles, but had suddenly forgotten our lines, so this take would end up on the cutting room floor. There will have to be another take; this one wouldn't do. The woman edged closer to him and quietly, sleepily asked:

"Who's this?"

"You've come at a bad time," he said at last, still holding the door. The woman eyed me up curiously. I was not invited in. Perhaps I should have gone in, who knows. Suddenly the air came back into my chest, my mouth opened and began to speak in an alien, reedy, metallic female voice, as the air left my lungs:

"Take me home at once. This minute."

"Very well."

Minutes passed, I hung around in the yard, peeked into the shed, in the scanty light filtering out from the house it could be seen that he had indeed been chopping wood and had indeed raked up the leaves. It must have made quite an impression: man with rake, maintaining his home. With a great big implement. He quickly got dressed while I opened the gate so he could drive out with the car. The woman didn't come to the window, though I thought she would watch us leave. Maybe she is crying, it occurred to me, though she didn't seem frightened. I didn't cry, seeing as I wasn't really there. The body that was allegedly mine, and now inhabited by two others in addition to myself, carefully closed the gate, let down the latch, got into the car, put on its seatbelt and said nothing. Not a word throughout the entire drive.

I'd never before seen him drive while drunk: we drifted from one side of the road to the other in the fog, at times almost leaving the road, and at one point we took a wrong turn at a junction and spent twenty minutes bumping along on dirt roads until we eventually found our way back to the highway. I did in fact speak, just once: I uttered a single, careful and chilly sentence, which included the unlikely word *echocardiogram*. He didn't respond. The car jolted us around, but we didn't die and by dawn we had reached Pest, where in front of the house he quietly opened the car door for me.

"What about you?"

"I'm going back."

I didn't put the key into the lock until the car had gone, and up in the flat I began to do quite ridiculous things. It was four in the morning, day was breaking, I put fresh sheets on the bed, lay down and stared at the ceiling with my eyes wide open. I still had the image of the little beds going around my head: I picked up where I'd left off in the afternoon.

I don't know how long I spent like that, I didn't count the days, I remember only that I stared at the ceiling in the same way in the hospital, as the doctor explained how I had to understand that because of the inflammation, the other one also had to be removed, we couldn't take any risks. A *large necrotic mass*, those were his words. It had to be scraped out, removed, cleared away. He didn't notice that I wasn't even there, that I was just cutting across the maize fields and waving back to my childhood friends from the edge of the dirt track. For some reason snow started to fall, the waiter came with a cup of tea. Not the waiter from Terenye, but a nurse. She pokes a straw into my mouth, though I'm at home and I'm going to get up in the afternoon. Many years must have passed meanwhile, because my face is old and ashen grey, my body is old and ashen grey, my voice is old and ashen grey, it's coming from the far end of the corridor opposite, but even from there it seems to be wrapped in several layers of gauze.

The autumn doesn't seem to want to end, is incapable of ending, the sun can't shine, and its rays only just about manage to penetrate the cold that is gradually taking over. When we arrive, my son and I, it's still October, admittedly its very end. Crows waddle to and fro in the frosty gardens, and someone has gathered some walnuts in a basket. I throw down my rucksack, the boy sits up in the tree. He likes to dangle his feet from there in summer, too, shouting into the house to ask me to make him some tea. I'm tired and my back aches from all the walking. I light the big brown stove, then without undressing lie down on the bed, wrapping myself in a rough woollen blanket until the house heats up.

The next morning there is a knock on the door. My son went down to the general store because it will be shut for two days. So it seems I've managed to lock him out. But no: the door opens and it's just the little girl next door who has come over. To check if the chimney was not blocked. Because – imagine! – at Uncle Antal's they found a dead owl in theirs.

I don't look up, busying myself with the stove. The ashes have to be cleared out, it must be cleaned of everything that has been burnt in it, so that the fire can blaze again once the inside of the stove has cooled down. I kneel down, reaching deep into the stove, but I can see from the side that the little girl isn't coming in and keeps glancing nervously into the house, talking all the while:

"My daddy has chopped some kindling, I've put it down outside."

"Thank you."

I don't know how much they know, I've no wish to speak with them. I've no wish to speak with anyone, I've specially pulled the phone out and switched off my mobile. I take great care sweeping up the ashes, but the little girl really will not leave.

"I tried phoning, too, but you weren't picking up. It always just beeps. They'll be having Hallowe'en in the village, for the first time. We can get dressed up. Auntie Ancsi is organising it, you have to go the house of culture for nine o'clock, that's where they're meeting up."

Meanwhile my son has returned, walking all the mud into the house. He puts the bread down, and they immediately start discussing who will dress up as what.

The girl finally shuts the door behind her. She is excited and in a hurry, she'd like to start cutting up the bedsheet straight away: she wants to go as a ghost. Or, even better, as an Egyptian mummy.

"Hey, what's Hallowe'en anyway?" she asks all of a sudden, because it hasn't occurred to her before.

"It's like the Day of the Dead," I tell her. "It's just that it's an Anglo-Saxon custom."

"What does 'Anglo-Saxon' mean?"

"…"

"What will you go as?"

"Me? I'm going as a witch."

I put the bread away and don't even notice that I've started humming the end of "The Witch Has Three, Three Kids Has She": *dum-di-dum-dee, dum-di-dum-dee…*

I stop suddenly, sit down in the kitchen, then pick up the bucket, take it outside, and slowly start sprinkling the ashes by hand around the outside of the house. The church bells are tolling.

WHAT'S THIS MARK HERE?

(BIKINI LINE)

This feeling of unease has been a defining feature of my entire adult life. I hated it all: the beach, the public bathing, the awkwardness of the sweltering bodies, the bleak shamelessness of all the bare flesh and the wrinkly folds and scraggy feet on public display, the unselfconscious buzz generated by the pathetic creatures. I hated the showers, the whole giggly, soggy scene, with the old women scrubbing themelves down with their backs to you, then turning round as they reached for their towel to reveal a mass of greying moss hanging down between their legs. I hated that there was such a thing as a body and that there was death, and that it was through the body that death spoke.

"My entire adult life" – says a talking head to the camera – "has been defined by the proximity of death." In James Moll's film *The Last Days*, Holocaust survivors attempt to recall their last days before being deported. One of the interviewees mentions a swim-suit. As a little girl this was what represented to her peace, Eden, freedom, the last time that body and soul were able to go swimming in the present without being repeatedly drowned by the past and the future. When the seashore could still be seen. This was what they deprived her of, for ever, her swimsuit with the ruffles. And to her this is what first comes to mind even today, when over there in America someone asks her about that other, lost Eden.

My first swimsuit isn't a swimsuit. It's a pair of trunks. At that age there's no big difference between boys and girls: it's just chubby, flat-footed kids' bodies running about on the sands. The sun shines. I'm crouched down by a wooden tub, blinking into the camera. It must have been lovely in the hot sand. I show the photo to my son. Mum, he says, that isn't you, that's a little girl. Indeed: am I really me? In the background a fleshy female leg in slippers consisting of two blue crossed strips of rubber: beach slippers. The legs belong to my grandmother, who would soon take a step or two in the water, pulling a rubber dinghy. We are sailing.

The second picture: we are sailing through the air. A swing on the beach, the shore of Lake Velence, 1973. Still in swimming trunks, no upper bodice. Two muscular, children's bodies, brown as toast, fly through the air side by side; their ribs are visible. They are grinning as they push the swing with their spindly legs. They are cousins. One is a girl, the other a boy, they are both wearing black swimming trunks. One has a willie, the other a pussy, which they show each other in the musty darkness of the holiday cottage. Across the window a railing in the shape of a sail, painted red and green; on the walls splatters of wasps. Babies come from a mummy's belly and get in there through the willie. So there!

The third picture: Romania, the shore of the Black Sea. A thin little body in its early teens, wearing a proper, much yearned for swimsuit. A swimsuit for a big girl. The top is made up of two red triangles, though there's nothing under them. It's uncomfortable. It's constantly sliding over to one side and has to be pulled back; it comes undone at the neck, and you can't tie it at the back on your own. As for the bottoms, they are itchy and just get covered in mud. The girl takes it off, walks into the water and rinses it out. You can't do that! You're a big girl now!

You're a big girl now, go and fetch it yourself. I set off, clutching a banknote. I watch the people sunning themselves. There are men playing cards, one has a hairy back. Children asleep under sheets, picnic baskets, fat women whose red shoulders show the the white outlines left by their swimsuit straps. The soles of the grown-ups' feet are yellow. Their heels are like cheese rind. I don't want to be with the yellow-heels. Two scoops, please, chocolate and vanilla. The hot concrete burns my feet.

The ice-cold rock burns my feet. It's a twenty-metre dash to the warm water pool: those who have swum the distance can stay for a bit. It's winter, it's dark by six, the light from the streetlamps pierces the sulphurous clouds.

Steam rises from the water, there is a mist whirling around the Pomona statue, hardly anyone's left in the smaller pool. I seek out the metal pipe and crouch down into the stream where the hot water comes bubbling out of the side of the pool. Staring at the swaying images of the tiles at the bottom almost lulls me to sleep. Are you deaf?! Line up! A couple of minutes later we're running again, get a move on! We cross over to the cubicles on the far side through covered, unheated corridors made of wood. At the end of the line I speed up: look how this one has nice little broad shoulders. And she's quite handy, too. Where did you get that pretty little swimsuit? My daddy brought it from the GDR.

Anita Kovács can't come today, because she's not allowed to swim. She's got her period. Anyone who's got her period is a grown-up, can go to bed with boys, and even have babies. Once I, too, had some kind of brown splodge, which at first made me think I'd pooed my knickers, but there was no smell. And then that was all, nothing more, no bursting with pride that that was it: in the changing room I specially positioned my bag so that the cotton wool would stick out, "not sterile, not for medical use", in case someone asked about it (What's this crap? Oh, nothing, I'm just *menstruating*.)

Oh, nothing, just something I've got. Sure you don't want to come? Sure I'm sure. They all move down to the beach, bags and towels swinging. I'm left by myself on the terrace and undo my full-length sarong. There's a four-inch gash on my shin and it's not really healing. I tried shaving my legs in the bathroom yesterday. Like when peeling vegetables, I managed to slice off quite a bit of skin. In the first few seconds it didn't even hurt and I just glared at the white furrow suddenly opening up amid the field of brown, which suddenly flooded with blood. Oh, fuck. I didn't even try doing my bikini line. Down below they've have been sitting in the boat ever since, rowing over to the beach where you have to pay, making thin furrows across the dark, shimmering water that closed slowly behind them.

What's this mark here? Oh, nothing. I shaved my legs once. Last year, it was. And this one here? Don't. Please. It's fine. Is your sunburn still bad? Take your top off, I'll put some suncream on it, okay? Hey, take it easy, for heaven's sake. Jesus. Stop messing about, someone might come any minute. Don't worry, this late there's not a soul around.

It's cold, I get goosepimples lying on the sand, with the plastic beach bag under my head, the bikini just beside me, above me the starlit sky, and inside me an extremely slow-moving, cold, startled teenage finger. More, more. It hurts. You'll never leave me, will you? No, never.

Sand in my sneakers, sand in my wristwatch; time stands still.

The years speed by, what couldn't have even been imagined before has shrunk to the size of a thin little booklet, filled with plans and deadlines. The concrete burns the soles of my feet, I try to stay in the shade. I'm wearing my mother's old swimsuit, as my own doesn't fit. My belly sticks out, round and taut, my navel has popped out and is showing through the shiny, dark blue material. The bra cups are pointy, giving my breasts a cone shape like those of fifties film stars, the only difference being that there's no wasp waist below. There's nothing sublime about it at all: I just shuffle about with a horrendous beer belly, the tiny life burgeoning beneath my heart – as people like to put it – seems to churn around at a nauseating pace, a twisted little rag turning round in the drum of a washing-machine. I stop and, with a quiet inward-looking half-smile, vomit into a litter bin full of paper trays and plastic cups.

I'm still nauseous! Don't worry, says a woman stroking my hair. I'm lying on an operating table, with a green bedsheet hung up before me at the level of my breasts. All I can see is the doctor's frilly cap, as it bobs up and down behind the sheet: in the old days in the Széchenyi baths the old biddies used to wear such cabbage-style plastic bathing caps as they did their laps with their heads held high out of the water.

It's choking, it's going to choke, it's got to be taken out.

The sheet hanging in front of me is quite unnecessary: the curved metal shade on the battery of LED lights above offers a distorted reflection of what's going on below. I can see the C-section, the blood, the gloved hands, the green blob that leans in from time to time – the cap on the obstetrician's head.

We're cutting you at the bikini line, says the voice.

We're off to have the stitches taken out. The doctor is quite old: he must be well over 70. As I survey my bikini line I get the feeling that either he has never seen a woman in a swimsuit or, if he has, they were wearing a one-piece costume, or the period in his life when such sights made an impression on him must have been the early 1970s, when girls with Charlie's Angels hair-dos played beach-ball in their geometric-print, high-leg outfits with broad straps.

It's healing nicely, just make sure you don't do any lifting.

Don't go on about it, I say in response to the invitation, even though J. is urging me to go. It's from *Cosmopolitan* magazine, to go to a bikini show, featuring next year's fashions in swimwear. I imagine the flawless girls sashaying gazelle-like down the catwalk, then my belly with the stripes the colour of mother-of-pearl as if I were weeping from my navel, as if the wind had carved little silk roads in the brown sand.

And anyway: I know what next year's fashion in bikinis will be like: just like France's last year. I can already see in my mind's eye the posters at the beginning of summer, with dumb little pigtailed Lolitas leaning against the wall licking their lollipops, in the geometric-patterned, high-leg swimsuits that they wore in the seventies.

I sit on the beach, the waves draw lines in the sand, then the water retreats to leave the tiny exposed dunes to dry out. As if the coast were mirrored in the sky, the clouds above also roll past in large, angular streaks; the wind rises. The beach slowly empties, the half-naked girls gather their things, shake out their towels, one of the Arab lads leans agains the concrete wall and shakes the sand from his sneakers: the bare soles of his feet gleam, as if he had dipped them in light. It's getting cool. Gradually I realise I'm on my own. I've been waiting for three hours, a fully dressed alien, while twice walking up to the will-o'-the-wisp of the telephone booth by the highway, and in the blistering heat, holding the receiver, stared down towards the shore. "Leave a message". Right, I'll just write it in the sand: "J'ai tant rêvé de toi".

I must get something to eat, and I've got to have a pee. The bus leaves quite soon.

I'm hungry and I'm tired, what else can I possibly desire: as I walk up, these lines rise to the surface of my consciousness, from that song by the rock-band called Bikini.

I LOVE DANCING

(DOUBLE WHITE LINE)

"A very decent fellow, that husband of yours," said Aunt Annus and gave me wink. The pieces of the green beans she was chopping up plopped into the basin with gentle thunks.

"Yes, very decent. Shame he's not my husband but someone else's."

Aunt Annus didn't risk a response, not even looking up. The little pieces she was cutting became more and more pointy, until there were none left. Soon, Zoltán soon came running in and together they put the sour bean soup on the burner.

Well, God bless, said auntie, shutting the door behind her as she went out. When we were on our way home to Pest the next day, we knew as we drove out of the courtyard that there were people staring at us from every one of the houses. We could feel their inquisitive looks fixed on the back of the car all the way to the motorway. The folk from Budapest. Friends of those lowlifes.

On the third or fourth time we were down at the little house the next-door neighbour again dared to bring up this matter, or blasphemy, as she called it. "Of course, you know best," she added quickly, "but it really won't do. It's pagan."

I reassured her that Zoltán had divorced the previous year and that we had every intention of getting married, indeed we were looking forward to having lovely children. I was only joking last time. This mollified her somewhat:

"You make some daft jokes, you lot," she said shaking her head meaningfully, then brought us a dubious looking jug of soured milk. The next morning she even showed us how to milk the goat.

"Like this, see."

I couldn't really make much headway and when on Wednesday morning she knocked on the door to say we should go and see to Mici, who was bleating pitifully, Zoltán came stumbling out in his boxers, grasped the surprised old woman by the shoulders and steered her out onto the veranda.

"Auntie Annus, we're just having a rest here, for fuck's sake. It's six in the morning," and drew the mosquito net tight behind him.

During the day the goat was tied up facing the street, not far from the garage, the roof of which Edit and her family had raised to the level of the garden and sown with grass. When she happened not to be grazing around the tree, she went up to this high point to survey the fairly unexciting dirt road. We didn't see Auntie Annus at weekends, though I did once catch sight of her back when I came out of a shop as she wobbled off on her bike towards the lower road. She took care of Mici, while we looked after the house, sprinkling the dusty courtyard with water every evening, and sat outside amid the ear-splitting chirping of the crickets. Summer was gradually fading: sultry afternoons would be followed by cool nights and shivery mornings, the grass heavy with dew when I stumbled over to the outhouse at first light. The house had no inside toilet and we regularly ran out of hot water, but even so, for us this was Paradise.

We would make love at dawn every morning, then sleep in until ten. The sun was already up when we woke, making the normally dull little mirror shine brightly on the far wall. Just now, though, it was still cool and misty outside when, still half-asleep, I heard someone tramping up to the front door and impatiently rattling the window. Zoltán immediately jumped out of bed, like a lover caught out: he pulled the door to behind him.

In the kitchen Auntie Annus was kicking up a dreadful row:

"Omigod, come quick, omigod, Mici's gone and killed 'erself!"

I pulled on a pair of tracksuit bottoms and ran after them in my slippers. The goat was dangling in front of the garage door. She'd gone to the very edge of the lookout and then, yielding to some mysterious impulse, hurled herself into the abyss, but as the end of the rope was still tied to the tree, she now dangled as if she'd been hanged by the neck. So not only could she not be milked, she was almost dead.

"Oh, for fuck's sake," said Zoltán, and set about trying to lift the creature up. I went over, too, and held her from the back, and together the two of us tried push her up onto the garage roof, but it seemed hopeless. When Zoltán let go of her, the rope gave a jerk and tightened even more around her neck.

"For heaven's sake, don't let go!" he yelled to me, but I was afraid Mici might summon up the last reserves of her strength to give me a kick or a bite, so instead I tried to reassure her by standing close and reaching under her rump. Finally Auntie Annus pulled herself together and came over with the suggestion that it would be best to try pushing a stool under the blessed creature. Zoltán went indoors and soon came out with a pickaxe in his hand.

"Mind out of the way!"

He raised his arm with such a backswing that at first I thought he wanted to kill poor Mici, but then I realised he wanted, rather, to cut the thick rope. This wasn't easy to do with the goat dangling from it: with each stroke the goat moved over a little, while the axe kept hacking little chips out of the door behind the goat, so that the paint came flaking off in large chunks.

"You're gonna to smash up the bloody garage door."

Zoltán stopped and looked at me as if about to slam the axe into my skull. The goat's mouth gaped open and it was clear she wasn't going to last much longer.

Auntie Annus nodded upwards with her head.

"P'raps we should 'ave a go from up there."

We both went round and while the old woman somehow clung onto Mici, now literally at the end of her tether, Zoltán hacked away the overhanging bituminous felt, and finally managed to cut the rope at the roof's edge.

The goat hit the street with a great big thump, and remained lying there.

The three of us squatted down beside her, trying to rub her side and bring her back to the land of the living, then hauled her into the courtyard on a duvet cover.

Auntie Annus left around 10 o'clock, with the reasssuring news that Mici had drunk a few drops of water and let herself be milked.

"Seems she's recovered from the trauma," I said to Zoltán as I poured the coffee. He was flipping through Edit's cookery books and just happened to be browsing *Masterpieces of South Slav Cuisine*. Garlic, basil. I turned pale, and lowered the coffee pot.

"You want to eat Mici?!"

"She's not going to recover," he said, turning a page.

I couldn't for the life of me imagine chopping up an animal, especially not a goat that was somehow part of Edit's family – it would have felt like eating one of our relatives on a summer holiday in the countryside. I went in to wash up, thinking that when I finished I'd go out for a while to spend time with the goat. Zoltán must have sensed how I angry I was, because after a while he followed me into the kitchen. I was just cleaning the recycling. Glass, paper, metal all had to be put in separate bins, and the kitchen waste had to be put in a bigger container, because at Edit's they had a compost heap.

"They throw all that shit together in the end anyway," he said, pushing the buckets aside with one foot.

He stood close behind me and begant to caress my breasts.

"Don't," I said, stiffening. "My hands are all filthy," and I raised my palms. He kissed them.

Some of the grime from all the cooking had lodged in the gap between the two doors of the cupboard, and it was on this sticky strip that a wasp landed immediately in front of our faces. It was twitching its little legs and vibrating its abdomen in its excitement. It must have found that strip so sweet, suffused with the smell and dried up deposits of a dozen summers. Zoltán didn't move, and though he suddenly loosened his tight embrace, he remained standing right behind me.

"Now watch!"

He slammed the cupboard door back at lighting speed: the wasp was squashed – splat – in the gap. At first I didn't take in what he had done but the moment I did, I moved aside in revulsion. He reached after me, but I pulled my arm away, picked up the four buckets and took them out into the sun.

Later I took Auntie Annus's three-legged milking stool and settled down in the shade beside the goat. She seemed to be alseep but under the rose-coloured eyelids that were open a fraction her eyeballs were in constant motion.

Zoltán came out into the garden from the veranda and began to fiddle with the garden hose, at one point spilling some water. He strode up and down aggressively, saying not a word to me, as if I weren't even there. After a while, without turning round, I asked him:

"And why did you have to do that?"

He came over at once and kissed my neck.

"It was fate. She wouldn't have lived much longer anyway."

His hand moved lower, clasping my stomach.

"I'm fat," I said. "Are you going to slaughter me too, like Mici?"

"Of course you're not fat, it's just the way you are sitting. You have a wasp waist!" he crooned into my neck and laughed.

"Idiot," I said, placated. I looked at his hand on my shoulder, as if it was quite unfamiliar. There was a strip of dirt under one of his fingernails, and a wound on a thumb that had got crushed in the swing bed on the porch. I generally gave this little semicircle a kiss, but now I just stared at it. I loved his hand.

On our way home in the afternoon the asphalt road shimmered in the heat, but we didn't have time to wait for the cool of the evening because Zoltán had some meeting in the office. I never asked him about such matters; the people in his stories were generally not known to me and had no part in the life we shared.

The sun was low in the sky and blazed down mercilessly. There was hardly anyone on the streets, with mainly tractors and vans turning out from the yellowing fields and only the occasional ordinary car. Then, after we left the first small town behind, traffic built up a bit. Zoltán kept twiddling the knob on the radio, then switched it off.

"You're very quiet," he said, looking at me.

"I'm sleepy."

"Anything the matter?"

"No."

"Yes there is."

There was a bend ahead, and I could feel that we'd crossed the double white line and suddenly gone over to the wrong side of the highway. He stepped on the gas and we suddenly speeded up.

"Stop that! At once!"

"Stop what?"

"Stop it!"

"Are you scared?"

The sweaty, tree-lined road was empty, with nothing coming the other way, but another bend in the road loomed ahead. He speeded up even more.

"Stop it!" I yelled at the top of my voice and grabbed his hand, but he didn't let the wheel be yanked back. He smiled.

"Say you love me."

"I love you. Daft prick."

We returned to our lane. Two seconds later another car came screaming out of nowhere.

"You're a lunatic! You're out of your tiny mind! Out of your tiny mind! Your tiny mind!" I sobbed steadily as I kept repeating the words. He took a box of tissues from the glovebox and with some difficulty pulled one out for me.

"Oh, come on, stop crying! You saw nothing happened."

I worked out that in five years we'd been down to the house thirteen times. After the accident, Mici got a shorter leash and Auntie Annus cancer the following year. Edit carried her over to the witch doctor in the next village, as she wouldn't take the medicines the doctor had prescribed. She died last year: her daughter told us how in her last week on earth she'd gone out onto the terrace in her nightie to deadhead the geraniums, cursing her son-in-law all the while for ruining her grapes. This was about the time that selective waste collection and piped gas were introduced in the village. And Edit and co. had a little room built on at the back of the house. This turned out to be the coolest place in the building: it was here that Zoltán liked to take an afternoon nap and to work in the evenings on a laptop on the small table; on occasion he even slept there. He claimed the place had a distinctive aura and it was where he got some of his best ideas.

At the end of May it was I who told him to ring our friends and that he should go and stay there for a while. Those days we met Edit and her folk less often: we would spend New Year's Eve together as always, but when in Budapest we hardly ever met up, though I knew from Auntie Annus's daughter that this year they didn't even go down to do the big annual clean-up.

I packed the tee-shirts and the windcheater, and placed beside them, wrapped up in a towel, a wasp-repellent light bulb to screw into the little lamp on the bedside table, in case there were already wasps about.

It was a long, hot week as the airless summer set in overnight. By Friday the heat engulfing the city was so overwhelming that even sleeping by the window I startled awake at dawn in the drenched bedclothes. It was five-thirty. I thought I'd go to the market so that we had everything in by the time he arrived the next day. Even the early morning sun was strong, already beating down on my shoulders as I left the house.

Back at home, I put down by the wall the basket piled high with bags of tomatoes, cucumbers, green peppers and apples, and went over to the phone. He picked up at once, though he was usually still asleep at this hour.

"It was awful to wake up without you," he mumbled into the phone before I could say a word. I was so overcome by the heat that I let him continue.

"Come back. You're being really silly."

One of the bags by the wall tipped over, the cucumbers fell out and some apples rolled out into the hallway. I didn't have the strength to put the phone down, though I was quite certain I should have done.

"Hello, hello," he continued in a whisper. "Edit, stop being silly, really. You even left your bracelet here."

I was in a daze as I clutched the receiver. Mechanically my eyes registered on the balcony opposite a woman with a ponytail in a yellow bathrobe as she put her bedding out to air. Somewhere you could hear the siren of an ambulance. Hanging into the corner of the window in the entrance was a branch of the sumach tree, as if it were a green pattern painted on by way of decoration.

"Hello! Say something. Forgive me, I didn't mean it like that."

Finally my fist unclenched and I was able to put the phone down.

The lecsó turned out to be rather tasty in the end. I made it with rice, because that was how Zoltán liked it. Then I had a look around the flat, because I remembered that there was an enormous, wooden bracelet, inlaid with mother-of-pearl, which I never wore and which for a while we displayed as an ornament on the dressing table, and then put away in one of the boxes of old junk.

On Sunday morning I heard his footsteps in the corridor outside. He walked with a characteristic, rhythmic gait. In fact, if the window was open I could tell by the way the gate shut that it was him, because he always gave the metal gate a shove as he closed it. He was here.

A person I didn't know entered the flat.

No beard, no moustache, hair almost razor cut. Only his eyes were unmistakeable, the rest of his face was like that of a close relative: almost him, but younger and startlingly alien.

I'd never seen him looking like this before. A thousand times naked, but never with a face that was bare. I know that men with beards sometimes shave them off, but he never touched his; he might occasionally have given it a trim with a pair of scissors, but shave it off – never. I stared at this new profile in the big mirror in the hallway, scrutinising it carefully. His chin was suprisingly round and slim, almost feminine, which gave his face a softer and chubbier look. He too was looking at me in the mirror and that was how we spoke to each other:

"It suits you," he said with a smile, looking at my arm.

"Thanks," I said and glanced at the big, chunky bracelet, which was more like an ebony handcuff.

An achingly familiar voice emanated from the alien face, so I quickly turned my back on the mirror and went into the kitchen. He called after me, almost teasingly:

"Could I have one last coffee?"

"Of course."

I set it down before him on the little table, two sugars and a spot of milk.

He kept stirring and looking down at the coffee, while I examined his freshly cut hair, the white skin of his skull, the curl of his ears, the palette of tones on his face suddenly caught by the sun. Where his beard had once been, the skin was red.

"And why did you have to do it?" I asked after a long time had passed.

"I don't know," he replied, and finished off his coffee. "I really don't know..." he repeated, spooning up the sugar from the bottom of the cup.

"She was a good dancer. And I love dancing."

TAKE FIVE

(FAULT LINE)

With great difficulty she managed to push the bed under the small, square window in the slope of the ceiling, so that she'd be able to see at least a little square of dirty sky when she lay down. But this made the space where the shelf had originally stood, at the end of the bed, just too narrow, so she carried that over to the other end of the room, by the writing desk. This improved the overall effect somewhat, though the room remained rather cell-like. Then she tried turning the table round, but that made it impossible to move in the tight space that remained, so she put the table back the way it was, and then paused to reflect on the scene. And the smell! There was really nothing at all you could do about the smell. It was a sort of sweetish mixture of the musty smell of the damp, mouldy carpeting and the oriental spices that remained trapped in the room, smells that had seeped into the now-yellow walls as a legacy of the three years spent there by the Moroccan girl who cooked on a hotplate. That hotplate, incidentally, had stood under the sloping ceiling, in the space where she had just pushed the bed, and as a result there was now an enormous splodge of grease right by her head. Later she covered it up with perfume ads from magazines, but it didn't take long for the reddish blobs of fat to show through the face of Linda Evangelista, and soon all the sheets were peeling off the wall. Why had the hotplate been put just there? Did the woman cook in a squatting position?

She must certainly have had to squat down to wash, as there was no other way she could have reached the washbasin: the place where the bowl had stood was clearly indicated on the spongy carpet by a ring of mould that was surely several years old.

And yet the Moroccan girl was probably right: when she had come back home for the first time she too had realised through trial-and-error that if she didn't want to have to carry the water from the basin too far, this was the only place you could put the bowl. Immediately below the basin it would be in the way, and it couldn't be put on the other side because of the door, which opened onto the corridor. So she put it back where it had stood before, adjusting it to cover the ring of mould. No matter, she thought, it'll dry out once the heating's on.

The little window barely gave any light, but if she now lay under it, stretching out on the grey, strange-smelling chequered blanket, she would nevertheless see some sky. From time to time an airplane would fly past, always diagonally across the window, from one corner to the opposite one. Birds were few and far between, almost as if there weren't any in this arondissement. Even at dawn, through the open window, all you could hear was the occasional wail of car alarms going off, or the sluggish creak of an early-rising neighbour's shutters.

The toilet was outside, in the corridor. Fortunately it happened to be at her end, so she didn't have far to go too far in her slippers in the dim light of dawn.

Apart from her there was only one man living in a flat on her floor. She knew it was a man because once, listening out behind her door, she waited for the toilet to be free and as she took a step outside she saw a pair of boxers just disappearing. But even from the way the door slammed she suspected that her fellow tenant was not a woman, though once, hearing steps thudding in the night, she had the impresion that a substantial, barefoot, black female was half-asleep in that attic room.

The postman never came up this far and regularly left Miklós's letters on the landlords' doormat. He always came between two and three in the afternoon, padded noiselessly up the thick red carpet on the marble staircase, and threw the pre-sorted bundles of letters out at lightning speed and with careless abandon.

If she happened to be home and ran down in time to the land-lords' door, she could pick out her boyfriend's envelope from among the bills and leaflets. Otherwise she always used the back stairs. The odours at the back were quite different from those by the main entrance with its annually repainted big glass door. Here the smell of the wax polish on the wooden staircase was overwhelming and mingled with that of the food that seeped out through the kitchen doors and with the characteristic stink of the household waste deposited in a blue bag by the door. Of all these smells the strongest was, in fact, that of the wax polish, and even years later if she was ever struck by this kind of waxy smell it would remind her of this creaky, winding staircase. For instance, fifteen years later, in London, she once bought hair conditioner with a label that had a little bee on it and when she opened it, her London bathroom filled with the odour of that staircase in Paris.

On their floor the smell was manifestly foul, especially in summer. As it spiralled upwards to the sixth floor, an atmosphere thick with the belchings of fermenting cheeses assaulted her nose.

They had no refrigerator, so the wheels of camembert were left by a window that opened onto the corridor. In winter, the milk was also hung out here, by means of a contraption made of knotted string, which made her smile, as they reminded her of her mother's macramé flowerpots. Of course these were no use in the summer, when the milk had to be bought fresh every day.

The store wasn't that far away, you just had to cross a busy road. She was capable of spending hours wandering the crowded aisles of Monoprix, only to end up buying tins of Bonduelle sweetcorn and frozen fish fingers, sometimes maintaining this dining monoculture for months on end, a diet into which a little variety was injected only by the various kinds of cheeses she bought. Once, at the cheese counter, she thought she caught sight of her fellow lodger, who was just carrying an enormous container of orange juice and a packet of muesli of some sort to the checkout, and she glared furiously at the figure in the windcheater and thought how he must be one of those health freaks, obviously keeping weights by his bedside so that after the early morning slamming of the toilet-door he could immediately set about giving his body some tender loving care.

Tender loving care was something that her body had not been given for the best part of a year. Whenever she hugged herself, sitting by the little window thinking of her young man, the images that surfaced were like stills from a film: Miklós in the corridor at the university, Miklós whispering to her in the dark, Miklós waving from the platform. Miklós was no longer a real being, just a sender of letters with news not from real life but rather as evidence of some sophisticated fiction, as if he were writing to and for himself, to prove that the body that existed in her imagination was not just a doppelgänger of her desires. Most surprising of all, she couldn't even recall his smell of his body. The other day, in one of the department stores, she had a sniff of every men's deodorant she could find, hoping that one of the sprays might summon up something of the spell cast by his flesh and blood; but what passed before her was only a parade of imaginary male bodies. Miklós continued to lack a face and was only a name, and even the address on the envelope seemed to be that of a made-up person, a fake address, Virág Cserép, 3 Föld Street, Hongrie.

She spent the whole of the previous day in the immigration bureau. She'd been summoned to appear at 8 in the morning, before breakfast. When she arrived and entered the barn-like 1920s building decked out in marble, the receptionist pointed her to the entrance hall. There was a vast crowd of people, some white, some black, and yet other, dark-skinned groups that seemed unclassifiable. They all kept looking around impatiently and if anyone went over to the chocolate or drink dispensers the porter reminded them in loud but measured tones that the examinations had to be carried out on an empty stomach. Nothing happened until ten o'clock. At ten-thirty an official appeared, distributed some forms, then disappeared down a side corridor. There was a sudden flurry of activity, pens were passed around, people filled in the forms in their laps, some translated for others, strange words, guttural sounds ricocheted in the air. By eleven, everyone was thoroughly exhausted. Black men took off their shoes, hunkered down one after the other on the floor, children burst into tears, women suckled their babies, while others strode nervously up and down in the side corridor, thinking that perhaps their impatient sounds as they walked to and fro might somehow get things rolling, or that they'd be allowed to go home.

At last, at eleven-thirty a stocky man appeared and led the pushing and shoving throng over to one of the corridors and, roaring at the top of his voice and gesticulating wildly, explained that the men must now split from the women, men to the left, women to the right.

Obediently they marched over Indian file to the lockers where they had to deposit all their clothes and inch their way along to the various examinations dressed in the paper gowns they had been given, each secured only with a piece of string.

There was a hold-up at the x-ray machines, because of an Asian woman shuffling ahead of her, whose stomach had a very visible bulge. Resting her slim, childlike hands on her little mound she looked at the official apologetically. Head tipped to one side, her face bore a shy smile, with something of the look of the deaf: obviously this universally expressed a willingness to cooperate – she's sending the message 'I don't understand you, but I am really listening, paying close attention.'

"Vous êtes enceinte?" came the question. The Asian woman, like a student caught out, just echoed the words: *Vous êtes enceinte?* The official became agitated and kept repeating the question at an ever-higher pitch as he pointed to the woman's belly. She looked back at the official with an emollient smile: yes, she said, baby. She, however, couldn't stand it for a moment longer and marched up to the official:

"Monsieur, can't you see she's pregnant? No x-ray!" The man shot her a venomous look, and motioned to her to get back in line. When it was time for him to take her passport, he started leafing through it with intense curiosity (goodness! so many countries!), his eyes eventually alighting on something at the bottom of one page. He read out the name: "Mlle. Hungary Magyar."

She'd have been amused if this had been the name she would bear on becoming a French citizen, but in the circumstances she felt obliged to intervene and so, moving awkwardly to maintain her modesty in the paper dress, she simply took the passport out of the man's hand and pointed to the correct rubric. If looks could kill, the pimply official would surely have murdered her on the spot, but in the event he just let her pass, and began to explain things agitatedly to the fat black woman behind her, who was trying with her chubby hands to hold together the paper gown bulging over her stomach and breasts.

Her blood was taken and her mouth and uterus peered into, with the details noted down so that some higher authority might eventually decide whether she represented any direct and immediate threat to the French nation.

When at four in the afternoon she finally was able to return, fully dressed, to the entrance hall, dizzy from hunger and exhaustion, she immediately hurried over to the chocolate vending machine. The Asian woman was there too, in a simple linen dress and sandals, with a grateful, permanent smile on her Madonna-like face.

"Where are you from?" she asked in English, her little bird-like head cocked to one side.

"Hungary," she replied, smiling back.

"Me too," the young woman nodded understandingly, and opted for a Mars bar.

It was getting dark by the time she reached home, at the other end of the city. The Monoprix sign was already glowing red and inside it was rush hour, with housewives pushing and shoving in the aisles with their trolleys. Exceptionally, she bought not only some sweetcorn, but added sour cream and some salad to the salmon in her basket, and then took a giant container of 100% pure orange juice and even a bar of chocolate. Hungry, me too.

She could barely carry the two heavy bags home. The container of orange juice snagged open one of the bags and she had to take it separately in one hand, so that when she got to the gate she had to put half of what she was carrying down on the ground. Fortunately, someone happened to be on their way out and let her in. Going up the back staircase she felt she was at the end of her tether, her only desire being to drop the bags and stretch out on the grey chequered blanket and watch the night sky through her dirty square of window. She unpacked by the door and started looking for her key.

She was struck by the smell of shit from the toilet. As she rummaged in her pocket, she thought with growing rage of the man who always slammed that door and decided that next time she'd buy a deodorant spray for the toilet: perhaps the jerk would take the hint. Meanwhile she had unloaded all her shopping and begun to turn out her pockets, which were stuffed with bits of paper tissue, but the key was nowhere to be found. She checked everything again, taking every item out of its packaging, though she already knew there was no point: somehow this was how this day was fated to end, the key wasn't there and never would be. She squatted down in the corridor, resting her back against the wall, and tried to gather strength. Changing the lock. The landlords. New key. Copy. The landlords are are away. Even if there is another key, no way of getting into their flat. Spare key. No. All she wanted to do was lie down.

Slowly she got up, and thought she might shoulder-charge the door, like Detective Columbo. It even flashed through her head that she might ask the man on her floor to help, but then she thought better of it: I'd rather break the door down myself. She took a couple of steps back, as far as the wall.

After the first charge, noting happened. The door shook, but didn't move. Fucking hell, thought Mlle. Hungary Magyar, and charged at the door with even greater force.

The doorframe didn't even shake. The green door's hardboard insert, however, suddenly came away from the batten. Right, one more go. With an appalling crash the insert broke away and through the gap that had opened up in its lower half it was possible to clamber into the room. She scraped her arm on the wood, but didn't notice. She went absolutely berserk, continuing to hammer away at the door from the inside until even the cross-bar gave way and only the lock and the doorframe remained. Through this gap it was now possible to take a step into the room, as if into some dark, oppressive painting.

She put the shopping bags on the table and lay down on the bed. It took a while for her to pull herself together sufficiently to nail the blanket across the doorframe: at least that prevented people from seeing into the flat. Then she lay down again and fell asleep in the clothes she was wearing.

She awoke to the sound of someone slamming the toilet door violently and saying something in front of the door that was obviously addressed to her.

"Next time don't smash down the door, fuck you! I have to work."

And why don't you use the toilet brush, you bastard, she would have liked to shout back, but this, too, she only managed to articulate later: at the time, lying there with her mouth gummed up with sleep and with her shoulder throbbing, all she could do was remain silent.

Incidentally, the man regularly left a streak of shit in the bottom of the toilet bowl. It occurred to her that she should do likewise, by way of response, an eye for an eye, a shit streak for a shit streak, but on the one hand she wasn't sure if the fellow would notice, and even if he did, whether he wouldn't identify it as his own streak of shit and then there would be no point; and on the other she was constitutionally incapable, on getting up from the toilet, of not using the toilet brush. Mlle. Hungary Magyar even dipped the brush in a little Domestos, which in the circumstances was of course a bit of a luxury, but it was a bit of luxury that she somehow insisted on.

Day was just breaking when she woke. She filled the bowl with water and got washed. It was as if the distinctive smell of the disinfectant in the aliens' bureau had somehow seeped into her skin and try as she might the soapy water made no difference to how she smelled.

She needed to have a pee, so she turned back the blanket and went outside. Leaving the toilet she was surprised to see that the door at the far end of the corridor was wide open. Somehow in the course of the past year it had never once occurred to her to go to the far end of the corridor, though there was a window there, too. She had a very poor sense of orientation and couldn't work out where the window down there might look out onto, whether it was the street, or some other part of the block. She was curious: the man's room aroused her interest. He was surely about to go away and was packing, and if she slipped past his door she would be able to get a glimpse inside without being noticed. So she set off in her slippers towards the open door. When she reached it she speeded up soundlessly, but when she glanced inside what she saw was so unexpected that it made her freeze in her tracks.

The room was much bigger than hers, but otherwise quite pleasant, with a beige carpet and rattan furniture. A double bed stood in the centre of the room. It was on this that the man was sitting or rather, to be more precise, the upper part of his body was lying, with his feet touching the ground. He had pushed down his boxers and in the geometrical centre of the room, like some totem or pillar of terrifying meat, there stood an enormous, erect penis. The man's eyes were closed, and he was jerking his hand up and down this gigantic, slightly curved organ and obviously didn't suspect that someone might be standing by the door. Or maybe he did. Who knows. Perhaps he did. Perhaps all this was being staged specifically for that person. Jesus. For a few seconds she stared at the the soundless body in the illuminated room, then turned round. She didn't dare go as far as the window now, but the next day she checked that what you could see was the roof of the house next door and, if you stood on tiptoe, a small strip of the side street below.

Returning to her room, she lay down on her bed with a pounding heart and touched her pubic area trying to recall the movements of the body of the being called Miklós. Miklós in the university corridor, Miklós in the dark of night, Miklós on the station platform. There was no Miklós: the images, as in some faulty projector, were continually overlaid by the startling and barbaric image she had just seen, the loathsome fellow with his closed eyes and gigantic curving cock.

The following week she didn't see him at all and the slamming of the door also stopped. Perhaps he had gone away. Thank God! The freak. She tried to work, but it wasn't going well. She had a short piece to translate for a guide book, that's what she was struggling with in the heat. "Budapest has a number of hot springs, thanks to the volcanic fault line that runs under the city. Budapest is a genuine spa city. The Hungarians are passionate about hot springs."

Miklós continued to write from the spa city, about the goings-on at the university, about how his exams had gone well, especially the one in sociolinguistics, that he would soon be going to the US, and the films he had recently seen. One of these happened to be showing in a cinema nearby, so one evening she bought a ticket, hoping in this way to bring the young man a little closer, as if they had gone to the cinema together, only at different times and a few thousand kilometres apart. Coming home from the cinema as she reached the sixth floor she heard a door just closing on the corridor. Since then she had had her own door repaired but the landlords still had not come back, so it couldn't have been anyone going into her room. In any case, they rarely entered the flat if she wasn't there. So it must have been the man. He must have returned.

She was irritated by the thought of the slamming door, which reminded her that she had still not completed the translation, and that she'd have to continue working in the sweat and misery of the attic room. She immediately put the deodorant out in the toilet, as a hint that could not be missed when he went to use it.

It was ten in the evening when she heard footsteps out in the corridor. Here goes. Summoning up all her bitterness she managed to rise from her desk and as soon as the door slammed shut, she roared with uncontrolled fury at the unseen enemy:

"Use the deodorant, you asshole!"

The man roared back:

"And you use your key, you stupid cunt!"

This made the blood rise to her face and she flung open the door:

"And use the toilet brush as well, you bastard!"

They looked each other in the eye and for a moment she thought the man would hit her. But he just took a step towards her and with quiet emotion said through gritted teeth:

"Crazy hysterical cunt."

At this she also went a step closer and raised her hand to hit him. He caught her arm mid-air and pulled her towards him.

She could feel from quite close the warmth of the youthful, sweaty body, and kept trying to hit him. Then she gave up. They set upon each other like wild animals, biting and kissing as the man began to peel off her panties and right there, in the corridor, holding her high up in the air, penetrated her. She didn't even protest, sinking into this strange vortex as if she had lost all her willpower to resist, as if it was an alien body deprived of consciousness that was writhing in the man's arms.

She was irradiated by an incredible joy, like an electric shock, and slumped down weakly by the wall, the man panting above her. She struggled up, pulling down her skirt. The man didn't say a word. They were like two students who'd had a fight in the corridor and were hurrying back to class as the bell rang. The man saw her to her bed and covered her with the blanket, as if she were ill and now needed to rest. In the way he tucked in the blanket there was a certain clumsy tenderness, an impression immediately undermined by the firmness with which he slammed the door shut behind himself.

She curled up under the warmth of the blanket and was surprised to feel, instead of a creeping sense of shame, merely a kind of replete emptiness, as if what had happened had taken place in square brackets, as if into a gap between two hot-tempered sentences an inappropriate, alien tone had insinuated itself. She fell asleep with her uterus burning as she squeezed a small pillow between her bruised thighs.

This same thing happened on two further occasions, except that they didn't tear into each other in the corridor but in her room, the same room that, on the first occasion, the man had helped her into as if she'd been in an accident. He had held her by the arms, as if it was her ankle that she'd twisted and not her brain. On the next occasion, however, there was no slamming of doors, no angry exchange of words: he simply knocked on her door. She opened it without a word, they rested their heads on each other's shoulders, like a couple about to say their goodbyes on a station platform after many years together, and then, with slow, increasingly passionate movements, began the act of coming together, the climax of which they both signalled with a high-pitched cry of passion. Not once did they exchange a word. The man satisfied her with steady and powerful movements, then got dressed and returned to his room.

She continued to feel no pangs of conscience as regards Miklós. The man next door was not an actual person, just an incubus, the kind that sits on the chest of a sleeping woman and impregnates her, and rains down curses on cows, so that they stop giving milk. A nameless apparition compounded of the noise of footfalls, tastes, smells, jerky movements; an incubus, a fleeting phantom bringing dark joy.

"I don't want to," her voice said to the phantom the next time.

"Yes you do," replied the phantom and slid between her legs. And it was true, between her legs she was slick and swollen from desire, betrayed by her body, as if it had secretly begun to serve the demon and to bend henceforth to its raw will.

One afternoon, on her way home from Monoprix, she caught sight of the man as he crossed the street, drawing his cardigan together as he was cold. Out here on the street he seemed taller somehow, and in daylight his features seemed in a curious way gentler and more attenuated. She quickly reached for her keys, to make sure they didn't arrive together. But the man ran ahead and opened the gate for her. They didn't look at each other, both embarrassed by the other's fully dressed body. The man went for the lift, so she headed for the wooden staircase at the back. He held open the lift door for a while, then announced somewhat formally, as if he didn't know her:

"Your lift awaits, madam." She nonetheless set off for the back stairs.

They reached the sixth floor at about the same time, but she waited for the door to slam and went over to the main stairs only when she was sure the man had gone into his room.

She wondered what that longish black case in his hand could be: obviously some musical instrument. Somehow this did not fit with the night phantom's determined, almost rough movements, though the face she had just seen in the light of day, with its furtive and distracted look, didn't suggest that it was totally out of the question.

In the evening, as she was about to go out, she saw that the corridor was full of big, black sports bags and various pieces of baggage all in a heap. The longish, black case, too, was there alongside them.

Without giving it a second thought she snatched it up as if it was one she'd left there by mistake, and at lightning speed slipped back with it to her room. She flipped open the lid. So, a saxophone. She sat on the bed contemplating the case, and thought how, as a matter of fact, she knew nothing about this man, yet their relationship was nonetheless governed by their original, latent antipathy, how he in fact despised her, that in truth he was just using her, that they had nothing in common; indeed, so much so that she was incapable of feeling even shame because of him, and that these were probably the kind of thoughts he had about her, if he ever managed ever to think of her body as that of a human being.

"Let me have it back," said the male voice by the door. So that's his daytime voice, when he is not whispering, choked with anger or passion: the clear, airy purity of his tone surprised her. She suddenly came to her senses, stood up and with as natural a movement as she could muster put the case out in the corridor. The man picked it up and took it downstairs. She could hear as the bags scraped the staircase wall.

Miklós hadn't written for two weeks. In the oppressive fog of her pangs of conscience and sleepless nights she imagined that perhaps he suspected, no, that he divined something of the growing distance between them, that the silence was to be interpreted as a question to which she was obliged to reply. She composed long and incomprehensible letters, cut off a lock of her hair, put it in an envelope and sent it off to him, and during the nights she tossed and turned as, covered in sweat, she reflected in the attic's ever-increasing closeness on their passion of old. And she tried to think of Miklós, of their lovemaking, the young man's almost courteous movements, as he articulated what he had to say in sentences invariably couched as queries to her.

Meanwhile the landlords had come back. She felt as if the sweat of many weeks was sticking to her skin, that in the evenings, crouching in the red bowl, she was no longer able to wash off the sourish condensation, that her whole body was filled with some kind of poisonous, vicious vapour, as if the seeds of some mysterious illness were growing in her groin.

She asked the landlords for permission to have a bath in their part of the flat. They were a little surprised, since the previous tenant, the Moroccan, had never made such a request, but after expressing some unease they relented. When they left again at the weekend, they gave her a key, with careful instructions not to use the washing machine if at all possible, and that she should carefully lock all three of the locks in the door that faced the corridor.

She prepared for the bath as if for a ritual cleansing. She ran the water, then added quite a bit of shower gel. She stripped and was about to step into the water when she suddenly remembered that she'd left her shampoo and hairdryer upstairs. The big old metal bath was only half full, so she left the hot tap on while snatched on a towel and ran up from the back door of the kitchen to her attic room. In seconds she was scurrying back with the shampoo and the hairdryer.

On her way down the back stairs she stopped dead in her tracks. She heard the door slam but thought it must be someone dumping rubbish outside. It wasn't. The landlords' door was shut. She tried giving it a shove. The key was inside the bathroom, under her clothes. Here she was, standing in the stairwell without her knickers, in just a towel. She was overwhelmed by a sense of hopeless exhaustion and, as if she had a stomach ache, slumped down onto the floor still clutching the hairdryer.

Suddenly the sound of steps could be heard, someone was coming up the stairs. She wanted to run back upstairs, but didn't feel she had the strength. Meanwhile she could imagine the bathtub slowly filling up, the overflow drain manfully glugging down the soapy water for a while before it began to spill over the side of the tub in tiny rivulets.

It was him. He stopped in front of her with his bags. He looked first at her, then at the door.

"Why don't you smash it down?" he asked with a touch of sarcasm. She was once again suffused with the dark fury of old, that here she was naked, in just a towel, and her anger did not dispel even when the man slowly put down the two enormous bags on the floor, amid the bath gel that had flowed out and, carefully placing the instrument case by the wall, called out to her:

"I'll go and get the concierge."

The water soon began to flow from under the door. It had obviously flooded the grey carpet of the entrance to the flat and was well on its way to the stairwell. The sweetish floral smell of the bath gel filled the air, and she could now feel her feet getting damp in the tufted slippers. "Budapest has a number of hot springs, thanks to the volcanic the fault line that runs under the city. Budapest is a genuine spa city. The Hungarians are passionate about hot springs."

Soon a noise could be heard from the other side of the door, the key turned and the man opened up. For a moment they looked each other in the eye, then she said:

"Merci bien."

Down on all fours, they mopped up the floor with the towels they had thrown down on it. Meanwhile she was trying to imagine what Miklós would have done in this situation. Would he have done anything at all? Would he have been capable of breaking down a door, would he have been capable of breaking her in, of mounting her, of accepting her without a word, or would he be forever satisfied with that walk in the park? Where, for Miklós, were the limits of passion? What words, if he were to see her like this, would they be able to say to each other after so many pointless letters?

They worked in silence, letting the towels soak up the water and wringing them out. She ought to ask what his name was, she thought, but then the idea of such introductions in this flooded bathroom seemed so absurd that she preferred to keep bending over and wringing out the towels. Soon the concierge appeared and in his characteristic Marseilles dialect began to express his regrets and to shift the bathroom chair awkwardly and pointlessly to and fro. The Monsieur, he pointed with his chin at the man with the rolled up trousers, because perhaps he didn't know his name either, or just because he considered it superfluous to address him by name in such a bizarre situation.

"There's a Monsieur" was also how he reported two weeks later that Miklós had arrived with a big suitcase on wheels. "There's a Monsieur waiting for you downstairs," he said, articulating slowly and carefully and pointing downstairs, as if unsure whether the girl understood him.

They had trouble getting up to the sixth floor, Miklós leaned against the staircase wall, panting.

"You are lovely," he said to the alien face.

"Merci bien," an alien female voice replied. "This is my room, here."

Now, as Miklós spent the whole day pointing to places on the map and asking her questions, she was forced to realise that, although she had lived here for more than a year, she hardly knew Paris at all. She had, for example, never been to the top of the Eiffel Tower – somehow she had never found herself in that neck of the woods. She was irritated that that was where Miklós wanted to go. She was irritated that he had brought his own shoe polish, and she was irritated by the way he bit into his baguette at breakfast. It was as if with his even, longish teeth he were chewing every bite more thoroughly than normal, as if some strange sounding-box were amplifying the noise of his regular chewing. I hate the way he eats, the volcanic sentence burst to the surface of her conscious, as she watched Miklós at the table from her position lying on the chequered blanket.

"Jazz clubs," the young man said loudly, and she should have confessed there and then that she hadn't been to a single jazz club all year, just as she hadn't been anywhere else, that since buying the red bowl she had hardly moved an inch outside the arondissement, that all the rotting cheeses in the window were hers and not the next door neighbour's.

"How about *Le Bœuf sur le Toit*? OK?"

"Yes," she said, it would be as OK as anywhere else, she added to herself, as she watched Miklós's back.

The man should enter first: that was the custom in places of entertainment, and Miklós invariably obeyed rules of this kind. There was some shuffling about with the chairs and then they sat down in a corner. They said nothing, then ordered a kir royale. Meanwhile a man with hunched shoulders passed by their table and with an apologetic smile and his head tilted slightly to one side placed a keyring with a heart-shaped bobble on their table with a note: "I am deaf, please help." Miklós placed the heart in her hand and gave her a knowing look. The banality of the act made her shudder, and she quickly said:

"Please don't buy it."

"What was that?" he said, turning to her, having not heard what she said, because the band had just struck up.

"Don't buy it!"

"What did you say?" asked Miklós, bending closer and gently brushing her hair aside.

"That!" she shouted into his ear. "Perhaps that's something you might do, sell these little hearts!"

Miklós smiled but didn't look at her, because he was already staring at the little stage, lit by a green light. But she was listening to *Take Five* and fingering the keyring with the little heart, and not daring to look at the saxophone player.

MISERERE

(DRAW A LINE UNDER IT!)

One way or another, even if it sometimes comes apart at the seams, the world is a web of often opaque laws, or of interconnections glistening like gossamer in the pale light of dawn, with the ends of each strand tied to a different corner of time.

At such times, in the early morning, the garden is all dampness. I stride through the grass in my sandals, my feet all dewy, the rose-bush by the path scratching my leg. I'm going out to the front of the house, I want to see the bodies. I'm approaching the fence, I'm about to press down the latch of the gate. Even from here, indoors, one can see that some of the legless torsos scattered in the grass are still moving, even though we have lived through a night seemingly without end. I too spent the night tossing and turning, unable to sleep, scratching the wasp stings on my bleeding legs and counting how many more nights I would have to spend in their company and with these friends of my parents, to me nonetheless quite alien and incomprehensible beings who filled with unfamiliar objects and strange smells the cosy holiday cottage that I had thought would stay the same forever. There are nappies drying in the garden and in the little room where I generally sleep they have set up a playpen for the twins. I have to share a bed with the big boy, stocky and bony, who keeps pulling the blanket off me and jabbering on about scary things in the dark, then pretending that he's asleep even though he keeps farting away quite loudly. It's not storks that bring babies, he whispers, and that was certainly not how the twins arrived. He remembers that when his mother came home, his pet frog died. Why did it die, I ask. Well, because my mother fell pregnant, that's why. She got a baby in her belly and and that's why the frog died. Two babies actually, he adds. It doesn't make any sense to me, but some kind of mysterious connection nevertheless formed in the back of my mind, to do with the stork which, though it doesn't bring babies, does eat frogs and so must be involved in some way.

If the gate were open, I could escape. I know how to get as far as the railway station: you walk straight down the mottled concrete pavement lined with cherry trees, all the way to the highway, as if heading for the beach, then turn right and from there you can already see the railway tracks and the whitewashed fence of concrete along them.

The twins are still asleep, though they are generally bawling by this time of day. I am the middle one of the kids, for the twins have a brother three years older than me and so old enough to go along with them on their nighttime fishing expeditions. I wanted for a long time to be able to go with them: half-awake, I often heard them getting ready to leave, then fell asleep again, only to wake a couple of hours later, when the twins began to howl. Then one morning they finally gave me the smallest of the fishing rods, saying here you are, off you go the pier to catch frogs. After the first flush of pride I immediately got cold feet. I couldn't find a red rag, so in the end it was the torn-off corner of a red plastic carrier bag that I pinned to the rod, and the lads said that would do.

The gate is locked.

They, that is to say Little Jani and his new friend, the one he'd just met and who brought a popgun from their chalet, were also hunting for frogs that day. They went down to the reedbeds by the water's edge and took aim at the flickering heads unsuspectingly floating in the sludgy water. If they got one they jumped up and down like mad and high-fived each other, then quietly waited for the green bodies to surface again. I stared at them from a distance and with one hand yanked the line to and fro, but the distant explosions made the frogs jump into the water one after the other. In the end, though, one did swim after the red of the hook bobbing in the water, and after following it for a while, unexpectedly gobbled it down.

"Got one, got one!" I yelled with a pounding heart, and the others started running along the bank, making the pier shake.

I hauled the body, twitching and jerking at the end of the fishing line, out of the water.

It was throbbing in my hand, its mouth agape, and seemed to be staring at me. I was suddenly overcome by a feeling of desperation and thought I should let it go back. Meanwhile the boys arrived.

"Get the hook out, you lame dork!"

"I don't know how."

"Here, let's have it."

The hook wouldn't come, they began to tug at it. Suddenly something white like crushed silk appeared in the open mouth of the frog, followed by something red.

"Hey, its fucking guts have come out. It's swallowed the bait."

"Leave it the fuck alone."

In the end the stranger took out a penknife and cut off the end of the line and flung the frog back into the water, hook and all.

"Take another hook," he said, offering me a small white box.

The frog turned on its back and then started swimming off sideways. Propelling itself with its muscular back legs, it would stop now and then, and resume swimming for a bit, until it reached the edge of the reeds.

We stood and watched. I even held my breath, praying silently: God help him, just this once, to make it.

"It will get better, won't it?" I said, turning to Little Jani hopefully.

He must have been a little ashamed of my whiny voice and trembling lips, so he only answered under his breath and turned away, seemingly addressing his reply more to another boy:

"Yeah, well, if they take it to A&E." They all guffawed and went back to their shooting, and I gave up fishing for the rest of the week, the rest of the year, for ever. No longer envious of those who rose at dawn, I preferred to hang around the garden in something of a daze, or to feed the neighbour's vizsla dog raspberries through the gaps in the fence.

The twins have just woken up, I can hear the comings and goings indoors. In a moment they'll get their cocoa from their baby bottles and when they've finished I am allowed to drink what's left. That makes me go out and sit on the terrace and think of my mother's morning cocoa, and count down the days I have to endure until they come home from Germany.

After breakfast the twins' nappies are taken off and they spend some time in their playpen on their tummies with their bottoms bare. Their muscly white thighs and scrunched up legs are a bit reminiscent of the frogs', and though it would be nice to stroke their fluffy, egg-shaped heads, it's not allowed, their mother explained, because their fontanelles are not yet closed.

Now she is standing out on the terrace and shouting in my direction with a baby's bottle in her hand.

"Well, aren't you coming?"

"No thanks. I don't feel like doing anything." There's been something in my throat since last night, something hot and sour that's making my mouth sting. When Big Jani and his family left first thing, I pretended to be fast asleep, even though Little Jani made a point of pressing his hands on my legs as he clambered out of bed. They'd be bringing some fish again in the afternoon, like yesterday. But yesterday it wasn't just fish that they brought.

I can't tear myself away from the scene ouside the fence, from the torsos scattered in the dust-laden grass. Aunt Ági shrugs her shoulders and goes indoors.

Yesterday Little Jani was waving a net around the kitchen, a net full of slow-moving frogs' bodies going round in confused circles. His mother yelled at him to take them outside for heaven's sake, whereupon Big Jani gave her a hug to try to calm her down. Come now, my dear, don't be making such a carry on, we're going to eat them. That's what the French do, so they can't be that awful to eat. Mon-sewer, silver-play, mon-dew. And he spun the net around in front of her nose as Little Jani grinned from ear to ear.

"Outside, in the garden! You're not going to make a mess in my kitchen!"

Auntie Ági gave the bag another disgusted look, then went off to see to the twins.

The fish were waiting in a pail: that day they didn't have pride of place. Big Jani was already unpacking the bags, while Little Jani was stoking up a proper fire. The next-door neighbour was standing by the fence and pontificating: not every kind of frog was edible, and we should be careful we didn't get any of their pee in our eyes because that could make you blind. The vizsla was running up and down by the fence, barking excitedly, as Little Jani had crouched down and was driving it to distraction with a twig.

"There won't be enough time," Big Jani said and went indoors to fetch a pan.

We sat on some treestumps by the fire, turning the skewers as we fried the bacon. Big Jani took a knife, put the first frog on a stump, and with two quick movements chopped off its hind legs. Then he did the same to the others, one after the other. He threw the bodies, still alive, into a plastic carrier and laid the frogs' legs out in the pan.

"Take the bag out into the street. The storks'll have 'em," he said to Little Jani.

Little Jani ran over to the gate with the pail and watched for a while, fascinated to see some of the bodies using their front legs to crawl off into the grass. Most of the bodies were still gawping, though not much could be heard from their throats. For some reason they all set off in the same direction, in so far as they were able to move at all: they appeared to be aiming for the far side of the dusty road, perhaps drawn by the damp exudations of a frog heaven that promised redemption, or by the shade of the bushes, or the memory of the distant pond stirring in their guts.

Mama Ági cleaned the fish, the twins woke up and started howling, so I lay down in the living room under the blanket and prayed to dearest God. I begged Him to help them, to tell the storks to hurry on over, so that all this could please, please, please be over and come to an end, trying to rock myself to sleep in the stifling heat and dark. My burning snot mixed with tears, birth with death, as blood, wooze and horror all merged into a cloud of sludge, and I was on the verge of falling asleep amid all my tears when Big Jani unexpectedly snatched the blanket off me.

"What's up? Not having dinner?"

I shook my head but couldn't manage to get any words out. Big Jani kept glancing outside uncertainly, plates in hand.

"Stop that whinging. What are you crying for? The reason you're so scrawny is that you don't eat. We'll leave you some fish." And with that he went.

For a time I could hear them talking outside, followed by Big Jani's histrionic spitting.

"Sheesh, sod it, it's shit. Heaven help me, it's shit." The neighbour guffawed mockingly, the vizsla barked, and the images from my dreams slowly merged with the garden noises that gradually lost definition. In the semi-darkness, on the border between sleep and wakefulness, there was the gleam of something of that gossamer-like web that managed in the end to keep together the centre that would not hold, a soft and supple web that would toss back into the world that scrawny child's body of mine constantly on the verge of slipping through the cracks of existence.

I didn't eat any fish, nor much of anything else either. Certainly nothing at all that week. My mother always said I survived on cocoa and fruit, yet somehow I still managed to grow up in the end.

And the twins, too, grew up, their pale frog bottoms becoming muscular male ones. As for Little Jani, he took the twins that were now his own for a walk like an overweight, well-built paterfamilias. Over the years a kind of numbed stupefaction stiffened the lines of Big Jani's face so that it came to look like a mask. He bore his frequent and ever more serious bouts of illness with a childish peevishness. He had already spent three years in a wheelchair by the time I persuaded myself that I had to visit him. It wasn't I who wanted to go, it was my parents who insisted. Somehow our relationship had improved since I'd got pregnant and they tried to capitalise on this by constantly invoking images of my childhood: this visit was, in fact, more a rapprochement with them, and they thought that even if there was no way back to the past, repeated mention of the those who had been a part of our former existence could strengthen those bonds between us that had become so loose. All the while, though, I was ashamed that even now, as a grown-up, I was unable to forgive and still went about my life burdened with the memory of those decades-old pains and the words that still throbbed deep in my breast, and I was incapable of forgetting, of re-assessing, or even of merely understanding, all the wounds inflicted on me. You have to draw a line under it, my mother would say, just draw a line, and that's it. From then on, all's forgotten. All right. But what kind of line, I wonder.

Entering the airless press of the living room in the council flat, I knew at once that I shouldn't have come. I didn't recognise that old man, and he certainly didn't recognise any of us, and hadn't for a long time. His wife and one of the twins stood on either side of him, and a glistening thread of spittle drooled onto the blanket in his lap. He had felt unwell in the morning. Miserere, his wife explained, that's the medical term for the dysfunction of the digestive tract that he suffered from. It's when the system grinds to a halt, becoming paralysed, and the contents of the lower intestine dribble slowly back up the digestive tract, and leave the body through the mouth. And she gestured with her hands to indicate how.

"Not to mince words, he vomits shit," said one of the twins turning towards me; I didn't know which one, because since I'd arrived their mother hadn't addressed either of them. Miserere, miserere, I repeated to myself and surveyed the wardrobes and the objects so familiar from my childhood: the striped china cat, the Margit Kovács sculpture. I wanted to give Big Jani a pat on the hand but I suddenly hesitated and just stood there lamely, a stranger, while the two of them turned his wheelchair to face the window. His wife wiped his haggard face down with a damp towel – not that this made much difference but she wanted to show she cared for him, to channel the irritation she felt about her helplesssness into dramatic gestures. Then they pushed back his backrest and I went out into the kitchen, because I saw they were folding back the blanket: it was the beginning of some kind of well-practised ritual that I didn't want to be party to. For a moment I caught sight of his improbably thin and flabby thighs, the lower half of the yellowish-white body shrunken to the size of a child's. Outside I almost stepped into the red bowl on the floor, stuffed full of rags. From somewhere down below came the sound of a radio. I wanted a glass of water: looking for a glass, I could see that the aluminium strip had everywhere peeled away from the side of the kitchen cupboard. The water was lukewarm, whitish, and tasted of chlorine. I just sat on the barstool, staring at the sun sinking slowly behind the outline of the tower block opposite. Please, just let this be over, let it pass, let that invisible thread tense and let that web glistening like a fishing line quiver, let that fraction of a second come when the swimmer dancing on the surface of the water disappears for ever. Because I knew that all this was just a question of seconds, hours, years, that all this was just a question of lives. That in the end that's how it will be.

FORTHCOMING TITLES

Jantar is an independent publisher based in London that has been praised widely for its choice of texts, artwork, editorial rigour and use of very rare and sometimes unique fonts in all its books. Jantar's guiding principle is to select, publish and make accessible previously inaccessible works of Central European literary fiction through translations into English... texts 'trapped in amber'.

Since its foundation in 2011, Jantar's list has been made up, mostly, of works of literary fiction. In 2023, we begin to broaden our mission to include works of science fiction from Central Europe, a region rich in authors and stories in this genre.

Being Jantar, we begin our new SF list with the first recognised works in the genre written in Czech and Slovak. **Newton's Brain** by Jakub Arbes and published in a new translation by David Short, was first published in 1877, 18 years before *The Time Machine* by H.G. Wells. It first appeared in English translation in 1892. Arbes was much admired by Émile Zola.

Our second SF title was written in an uncodified version of 'Old Slovak' and published in 1856. **The Science of the Stars** by Gustav Reuss is arguably the first title to feature a balloon travelling to the moon. It is certainly the first to appear in any version of the Slovak language.

Also coming soon is the much-anticipated new translation of **The Grandmother** by Božena Němcová. Together with Erben's *Kytice* (Jantar 2014) and Mácha's *May* (Jantar 2025), **The Grandmother** is one of the three foundational works of modern Czech literature. This new and complete translation by Susan Reynolds will show, for the first time to English-language readers, the subversive, feminist, anti-theological and anti-Habsburg elements in this classic text. It will be published in a regular prose version and another illustrated by Míla Fürstová.

These titles and all our other titles can be purchased
postage-free world-wide from our website:
www.JantarPublishing.com

SELECTED TITLES PUBLISHED BY JANTAR

Barcode is one of many collections of short stories published by Jantar in English. In 2022, we published **DEAD** and **Mothers and Truckers** by Balla and Ivana Dobrakovová respectively. Another, very popular, collection of short stories was published in 2018 called **And My Head Exploded**. Featuring 10 shorts stories, the book features the work and authors from the Bohemian fin-de-siècle era never previously translated into English.

In 2017, we published **Fox Season** by Agnieszka Dale, a collection of dazzling stories set in a London bracing itself for Brexit. It is now making its first appearance on university literature courses. The stories were described by Zoë Apostolides in the *Financial Times* as 'fascinating and refreshingly honest stares at life in a foreign place, whatever that definition might be.'

City of Torment by Daniela Hodrová, published in 2021 attracted very positive reviews in *The Los Angeles Review of Books*, *The Irish Times* and *New European Review*. The book begins, 'Alice Davidovič would have never thought the window of her childhood room hung so low above the Olšany cemetery that a body could travel the distance in less than two seconds.'

The Birds of Verhovina by Ádám Bodor features a cast of weirdos and miscreants left to make their own way in the Carpathian Mountains. It was described by Diána Vonnák in *The Times Literary Supplement* as 'one of those places you might visit but might never leave; it is reality on its way to becoming allegory.'

Carbide by Andriy Lyubka was published at the end of 2020 when we all thought the worst that could happen was to be locked-down by a global pandemic. Set in what now appears to be the very quaint Ukraine prior to its attempted evisceration by Russia, Lyubka describes another Carpathian periphery world populated by criminals, corrupt local officials and a delusional history teacher. *Carbide* was described by Kate Tsurkan in *The Los Angeles Review of Books* as 'a fast-paced tragicomedy which establishes the young author as Ukraine's modern-day Voltaire.'

These titles and all our other titles can be purchased
postage-free world-wide from our website:
www.JantarPublishing.com